Amber Eyes

The Club Red Series

Book 3

By Aurelia Yates

TABLE OF CONTENTS

Acknowledgment

Thank you to Brent, Beth, Sam, Jackie, Nichole, Nikki, and my team, The Black Opal for your support. All the booktokers for their support. I couldn't do this without you. I'm so grateful for you. I also want to shout out to the ARC readers for Amber Eyes. I'm truly amazed on how many we had signed up and I want to give you a BIG Thank you for your support!

Love to all!
Aurelia

Follow Aurelia on

https://www.goodreads.com/author/show/22689072.Aurelia_Yates

https://www.bookbub.com/profile/aurelia-yates

https://www.facebook.com/aureliayatesauthor

https://www.instagram.com/aureliayatesauthor/

https://www.tiktok.com/@aureliayatesauthor

WARNING

This book is rated R; not appropriate for readers under 18 years of age; contains elements of sex, language, murder, death, violence, loss of a love one, abuse, spanking, consensual content.

PROLOGUE

Wiping my sweaty palms on my cotton skirt, I'm so nervous. I try to take deep breaths to ease my nerves, but it's not working. I'm on the verge of a panic attack.

I stand in front of a red steel door. Regret settles in my bones. I don't want to take this job, but I have no choice. I'm broke and need money to provide a safe place to live.

Currently, I'm staying with my friend, Carla. I was lucky her dad let me move in with them, but there's something about her dad that sends shivers down my spine. The way he brushes up against me and says inappropriate things makes me uneasy.

I raise my unsteady fist and knock on the door. When a large man with sapphire eyes opens the door, I swallow. Instincts tell me to run, but my feet stay planted like heavy lead.

I'm here to talk to Candy Mann about a job. I met Candy a few weeks back, and we discussed my living situation. She told me she manages the girls at Club Red and that I could make a better living working for her than waiting on tables at a five-star restaurant.

"I'm here to see Candy Mann." My voice comes out uneasy.

He looks me over, and goosebumps run up my arms. His eyes make me feel exposed.

Can he see my insecurities? My inability to feel like I belong anywhere?

He pulls the door open and stands aside to allow me to enter. Once I'm inside, he closes the heavy door, shutting it with a loud clap of thunder. Pure darkness replaces any light there is.

Darkness. That's all I have ever known.

"Follow me," he says in a deep accent.

My eyes adjust to the blackness just enough to make out the man's silhouette. Following him down a hallway, I see a sliver of light shining onto the floor.

He stops at the door, where the light shines through a crack. I bump into his back, waiting for him to say something, but there's only silence. He twists the knob to open the door, and the brightness that greets us is almost blinding.

The beautiful room we walk into has dark wood trim along the stage, where a gorgeous redhead is dancing on a pole. It's breathtaking. The red velvet curtains hanging from the walls give the illusion of long windows and pair perfectly with the crystal chandeliers hanging from the high ceilings that the bright lights bounce off of.

We walk farther into the beautiful room, stopping at a bar. The dark stranger doesn't speak. He reaches behind the red mahogany countertop and picks up a phone.

I'm not able to hear what he's saying on the phone because the music is loud. So, I watch the girl on the stage dance around, amazed at her confidence.

She's dressed in only a fancy set of underwear. Men in expensive suits sit around, watching her with lustful eyes as they shove bills into her tiny, barely-there panties, paying her to give them attention.

Someone taps on my shoulder, causing me to jump.

"Liz Black, you decide to take me up on my offer?" Candy says.

"Yes, can we talk more privately?"

She motions me to follow her, and we walk to a staircase and up two flights before she opens a door. We're greeted by two men in black suits.

Both men are tall and well-built, but the one standing in front of me with premature salt and pepper in his beard has a wickedness about him.

His dark, piercing amber eyes penetrate me, leaving scars as they sweep over my skin. A sudden icy chill breeze swirls around me. I brush my hands over my arms, trying to warm them.

I'm used to low-life drug dealers, but men in power suits that could make you disappear without question are deadly.

Candy introduces me, but my mind is too far from the conversation, so I don't hear their names. I give them a nod, wishing this brief encounter would be over.

When I tilt my head to the man with piercing eyes, he displays a sinful grin.

I'm ready to tell Candy this is not a good idea and that I don't belong here, but it's not a choice I have. I need the money, and if selling my virginity is what I need to do, then so be it.

Fairy tales don't happen to girls like me.

I slip my feet into the black stilettos I plan to wear for my first night at Club Red.

I'm only eighteen, but I'm taking tequila shots, hoping it will ease the pain of what will come later tonight. I throw another shot back, letting it burn as it slides down my throat.

Looking in the broken full-length mirror, I'm wearing more makeup than usual, with less clothing than normal.

Carla has already left to meet her boyfriend, so it's just Carla's dad, Mr. Camp, and I left in the house.

I always do my best not to be caught in the same room alone with Carla's father. The way his lingering eyes rake over me always fills me with dread. The fear of him pinning me down with his oversized sweaty body hovering over me makes bile rise up my throat.

Opening the bedroom door, I scan both ways down the hallway, hoping to avoid Mr. Camp. The air lightens when I don't see him in sight. From the bedroom, it's a clear shot to the back door, where I hope to make a silent exit from the house.

Stepping out onto the old scratched-up wood floors, I walk softly, trying my best not to click my heels on the hardwood.

When I make it to the back door, I stretch out my hand to turn the knob, but suddenly, I'm grabbed from behind and shoved up against a beer belly. It's him — Mr. Camp. I smell the stench of the cheap beer that he indulges in and sweat.

"You look like you're going to whore yourself out. I'll pay you if that is what it takes for me to get a taste of this pussy."

He slurs the words into my ear.

I try to push him off me, but he's much larger. His hand moves to my blouse, ripping the one-shoulder top.

I scream out as I try to hold my top up, but there's no one to hear me. Wiggling, I'm able to break out of his embrace. I run but make the mistake of backing myself into a corner of the kitchen. He realizes I'm at a disadvantage and lets out a taunting laugh.

Standing behind the kitchen table, I try to put distance between us, but he taunts me like a predator with its prey, matching my steps and movements.

Seconds go by before he charges at me. He comes so close, I feel his fingertips brush my skin. Turning, I close my eyes tightly and knee him in the dick as hard as I can. When I hear him grunt with curses leaving his mouth, I open my eyes to witness him grab his crotch and fall to his knees on the filthy floor.

Not sparing a second longer, I pick up my purse and run out the door as he's screaming for me never to come back.

I climb into the waiting Uber with tears staining my face, ruining my makeup.

When will this end? When will I be able to leave this life and find happiness?

When the driver pulls up in front of Red, I look out the window and see an opportunity, a new job that awaits me, a new destiny. This job is a means to an end. The end of a life that I battle each day, trying to keep myself away from the darkness of wicked games and drugs battling to win your soul.

I open my door, determination settling in. I'm going to get away from this life. I'm not going to be like my mother. I will not allow myself to be broken.

Squaring my shoulders, I knock on the front door of Red. The same man with sapphire eyes opens it. We don't speak. He just motions me to enter.

Once I'm in the door, he leads me to the bar where Candy is sitting. She has a drink in one hand and two young men at her side. Candy is a woman who knows what she wants and gets it.

My new mission—that's going to be me, a woman who knows what she wants and gets it.

"Hello, Candy," I project, my voice sounding confident.

"Darling," she gets off the bar stool and kisses my cheeks.

"Come, follow me." She leads me up a staircase. "I'll show you to your room. Each night you work, you will go straight there. You can freshen up there and put your things away in the locker in the room."

I swallow.

Am I really doing this?

Candy leads me down a hall. The décor resembles the rich decorations that are the same as downstairs. We stop at a black door that reads the number seven.

Lucky Seven. Let's see how lucky room seven really is.

The room is elegant, filled with beautiful furnishing. There is an enormous chest on the opposite side of the wall from the door and a gigantic bed with covers turned down. My insides tighten when I notice the white silk sheets. The irony of pure white sheets leaves bitterness on my tongue.

"Well, I will leave you to get comfortable, and just remember, if things get out of hand and we need to escort anyone out, just hit the emergency button, and security will be here."

"Thank you," I reply, my voice on the edge of breaking.

Candy leaves, giving me time to build myself up.

I can do this. I can do this.

There's a knock at the door. I square my shoulders, walking to the door, trying not to trip over my feet in these damn stilettos. Opening it, my ankles become weak, and I have to use the doorknob as leverage to hold myself up.

A large man stands in the door frame with bright, shining amber eyes, making the temperature of the room scorching. He doesn't wait for an invitation as he walks past me to sit in an armchair in the corner.

"Get on your knees and crawl to me," he commands with a deep accent.

CHAPTER ONE

Liz

Eight Years Later

I wasn't going to do this. I wasn't planning on walking or taking part in my college graduation ceremony. I simply wanted to receive my diploma and run. Start a new life in a new city. A place where memories don't linger and ghosts don't haunt me.

Carla's ghost.

Rose Sterling has been my best friend since we started working together at Ross and Asher Law Firm. I would do anything for Rose. That's why I'm here. Rose begged me to join in the ceremony, making me feel somewhat guilty for not celebrating this day. A day that I've worked so hard to make happen.

Someone with a past such as mine shouldn't be here today. I should be lying beside my friend Carla in a dark, cold grave at Hillsdale Cemetery.

Yet here I am, standing in the gymnasium's hallway, waiting for the music to begin, waiting to march across the large wooden gym floor to our seats.

Excitement doesn't fill me. Instead, there's an emptiness inside. It's the feeling I get every time I see two lovers together or a mother and father with their children. It's the feeling of losing my grandmother and Carla. It's the feeling of being alone.

I peer over at Rose. She's smiling at Blaze, who's sitting across from us in the gym. They both have lovesick expressions on their faces. The look I hope to have one day.

Blaze and Rose complement each other well, but the people he associates with are dangerous. I've seen high-rank mafia leaders come and go through the doors at Red. I know the men at Red—Wilder, Blaze, and Mark—do the money laundering side of the business.

They also have their own side hustle, making money being loan sharks. They loan out money to individuals with interest, but things take an ugly turn when customers don't pay within a time frame.

Being associated with men with ties to the mafia is not what I want. I've kept my head down and my mouth shut to survive. I don't want to be tied to a man who associates himself with people who are in the mafia.

Living in this lifestyle is a means to an end for me. I only worked at Red because the money is good. It's enough to provide me with a safe place to live, food on the table, and not worry about what I was coming home to each day. I couldn't count on my mother to take care of me.

My mother was a woman who couldn't say no to drugs. Frequently, she'd tried to sell me to her drug dealer. If it wasn't for my grandmother, she would have succeeded.

My grandmother took me in from age six and raised me until she passed. I was thirteen when she died and left me. Still too young and having no one else, I returned to live with my mother.

Every day, I fought to keep myself pure. To keep her from

letting random men touch me. She didn't care about anyone or anything as long as she got her fix.

When I was seventeen, I came home to our small apartment that always smelled like piss and reeked of meth. My mother was lying passed out on the living room floor—naked. Her boyfriend, Jerry, was pulling himself out of her.

When he saw I had walked in, he grinned, looking down at his small dick, as if I was supposed to be impressed by it. Quickly, I went to my bedroom only to have him follow me.

He said he wanted to ask me how my day was and if I enjoyed school. He patted the mattress for me to sit beside him, and when I did, he pulled me back onto the bed and climbed onto me.

I can still feel the tremble of my body, the feeling of his hot breath on my skin, licking and sucking the sensitive flesh of my neck. It still gives me chills to think about that day.

The adrenaline of being pinned down sent my mind spiraling. Those actions are what saved me from being raped that evening.

When I finally pushed Jerry off, leaving him to deal with his own blood, I ran as far away as I could, never looking back.

I lived with friends until I started working at Red. Hard work, saving my pennies, and focusing solely on my future have helped me get where I am today.

There's just one problem—Mark.

I can still hear the words he whispered in my ear after we fucked for the first time.

"Your pussy only has one thing to do, and that's to please me. No matter where you go, I'll find you. There is no hiding, *M'Aingeal*."

When the music starts, I bring my focus back on marching across the floor, and I spot the devil himself—Mark. He's taking a seat next to Blaze. The sight of him heats my skin.

Why does my body betray me?

Mark has kept me as his personal harlot—a kept secret—coming around only when he needs to get off. It sickens me.

How did I get this weak?

Shaking the thought from my head, I keep my eyes on the girl's head in front of me.

***

The last student is called across the stage. We stand as the dean of students gives his speech, then shouts of joy bounce off the steel walls as we throw our caps up in the air.

Everyone goes to their loved ones for congratulations. The sounds of cameras snapping pierce my ears. I have no family. I have no one to celebrate this day with, no one to memorize this moment in time.

I stand like a statue, watching Rose kiss her family. I admire the love they exchange.

"M'Aingeal," a dark voice breathes into my ear.

That voice has been whispering in my ear for too long.

Rose smiles, and her eyes find me as she walks over.

"Are you coming to our house for the after-party?" Rose asks with pleading eyes. "Please."

Pressing my lips together with reluctance, I ponder the question. Rose and her boyfriend Blaze share a penthouse together.

"I have ..." Stuttering, I try to come up with an excuse not to go. "An early day tomorrow. I won't be able to stay long." I feel contrition for the lie.

Feeling my skin burning, I hook eyes with Mark, whose facial expression is the same as usual—unreadable. No matter where he is in a room, my eyes hunt for him on their own accord.

"Will we see you, Mark?" Rose asks with an excited tone.

I wait on edge for his reply.

Mark's Irish accent is thick when he replies. "I have work to attend to, but then I will be there." He puts his hand on the small of my back as he moves past me, whispering in my ear, "I think you're wanted at work." His hand slides down to my ass, giving it a squeeze.

When he walks away, I expect Rose to mention him touching me, but she doesn't. I say a silent prayer that she didn't notice.

I don't want to explain to Rose that Mark and I have been fucking for eight years. Eight years of him not asking me to be his girlfriend, not wanting to introduce me to his family. I don't want to face my friends. They're happy in their relationships, and I'm not able to date anyone without Mark threatening to kill them, yet he doesn't want a relationship with me.

Sarah, who's been Rose's best friend since they were in middle school, comes to our circle with her baby on her hip. Sarah is married to Wilder, the owner of Red.

"Sarah," I reach out for her baby girl. Aurora looks so much like her daddy. She's got beautiful emerald eyes and strawberry-blonde hair.

"What's next, Liz?" Sarah asks.

"What do you mean?"

"You didn't take the job our boss offered you. So, I was wondering what you plan on doing now that you have your law degree."

I shrug my shoulders. "I haven't decided… yet."

I hate lying to my friends, but I know if I don't, I won't be able to get away from Mark, and I need to. I want to be in a normal relationship with an average man.

If I tell Rose and Sarah, I'm afraid they'll spill my whereabouts to their men, Wilder and Blaze, and it'll get back to the one person I don't want to find me—Mark. My body craves his touch, but my heart doesn't want to be around the dangerous lifestyle he lives.

The valid date for working as a sex worker for Mark has finally expired, and I plan to run as far away as possible.

CHAPTER TWO

Liz

I stare at the street below. I'm standing in Rose and Blaze's swanky penthouse. Their apartment is over-the-top ritzy, from the abstract rugs to the crystal light fixtures to the quartz countertops. There's no spot untouched with high-end furnishings.

Soft music plays in the background, and laughter is in the atmosphere, but my thoughts are of Carla. We dreamed of attending college together and moving away from New York City.

I close my eyes, and images of Carla flash through my mind. I remember the night Carla died. As I walked out of Red and headed home, an overwhelming feeling pulled me to the large metal dumpster, where I spotted a leg peering out of old crinkled newspapers. I ran back inside to get help. When Blaze came outside, he uncovered the face of the body, and I screamed. I screamed so loud and hard from the pain that shot through to my heart.

Carla was lying half naked with a needle lodged in her arm, her shorts and panties pulled down to her ankles. I still can't believe it's been eight years. The police ruled it as an overdose.

They said she was just another kid who didn't know their limits, but I knew Carla, and she never used drugs. She wouldn't touch them.

Carla was supposed to be with her boyfriend, Harrison, at his friend's house, listening to music as they normally did on a Friday night. She wasn't supposed to be anywhere near Red.

I inhale and blink rapidly to hold the tears at bay.

Rose's mom, Mrs. Sterling, appears from my peripheral vision and pokes my arm. I quickly try to swipe any runaway drops that may have escaped my eyes.

"Are you excited about graduation being over?" she asks sweetly.

I'm only able to muster up a half smile. Rose's parents have treated me like one of their girls from the first time Rose introduced me. I envy Rose. She has a life with her family that I've always dreamed of having.

I'm about to speak, but I stop when I see Mark walk into the apartment. His hand rests on the back of a gorgeous young woman with long, jet-black hair. My heart aches with jealousy.

I'm just his dirty secret.

I shake off the insecurity. We're just fucking, nothing more, but why does it feel like a betrayal?

I reflect on my conversation with Mrs. Sterling. "Yes, I'm excited to be done. It's been a long time coming."

Mrs. Sterling reaches out to hold my hand and gives it a squeeze. Reassurance, that's what it feels like. She always knows when I'm unsettled over something.

"Come on, let's go get some of that delicious-looking cake. You shouldn't be standing here by yourself."

Giving her a soft smile, I follow behind her to the large dining room where the cake is lying on an old-world charm rectangular table. The cake reads 'Congratulations, Rose and Liz.'

My face falls as I think about leaving and telling Rose goodbye.

I should reconsider and tell Rose about my plans.

When she cuts the cake, the fragrance of fresh strawberries reaches my nose. I close my eyes and inhale, letting a moan slip out. I'm enjoying the smell of the strawberry cake when soft, warm lips press against my earlobe.

"I know what else can make you moan like that." It's the same deep voice that's been whispering in my ear for too long —Mark. His hand wraps around my wrist. Just his touch lights a fire under my skin.

"Do you mind if I borrow Liz for a moment?" Mark asks Mrs. Sterling.

Slowly, I pull out of his hold.

"I'm sure,"—I look him in the eye—"whatever it is, can wait. Mrs. Sterling was so kind as to cut me a slice of cake."

With his eyes narrowing, he grips my upper arm, squeezing it hard.

"This is work-related." Leaning over to whisper in my ear, he continues, "I'm not giving you a choice, *M'Aingeal.*"

M'Aingeal.

I shake my head.

"Where's your date?" I bite out.

Mark's nostrils flare, "Liz." He says my name as a warning.

Mrs. Sterling watches the intense moment between Mark and me. I can tell she's not sure what's happening between us.

Mark and I stare intently at each other, neither of us willing to break our gaze.

"I'm going to check … to see if Rose needs me," Mrs. Sterling says as she walks out of the dining room.

Mark's eyes sweep down to my breasts, where a hint of cleavage is showing.

I tug at the top to cover myself completely. I shouldn't feel the need to cover myself. He's seen everything on more than one occasion, but I'm annoyed that he brought a fucking date to Rose's party.

Leaning in so close to my ear, he says, "I need to taste you." He licks the length of my neck. "I'm leaving for a few days, and you need to remember who you belong to. Be ready,"—he glances down at his watch—"in an hour. If you're not at Red ... naked, I'm coming to find you."

His words have my body already clenching, anticipating his enormous cock fucking me.

Fuck! I hate how his words make me ache for him to be between my legs. Fuck, fuck.

Shaking my head to clear my mind, I wonder if he has forgotten he brought a date tonight.

"In case you didn't get the fucking memo, I'm not working tonight." I jerk my arm out of his hold. "Get your date to suck your cock tonight."

I'm pushing him, but I don't give a fuck. He clearly thinks I have low self-esteem and that I will suck his cock after flaunting this woman around me. Well... he's going to learn today that I'm not the type of woman he can continue to use as his dirty little secret.

The edge of his lips rise, displaying a cocky grin.

This son of a bitch. Why does he have to be so fucking good-looking?

Before he can react to my outburst, his date approaches him, giving him a look of affection. In the next second, his mask slides into place with a soft smile.

I use the moment to my advantage and slip out of the dining room, leaving the penthouse altogether. I don't want to witness any moments of tenderness exchanged between Mark and his mystery date. He can go fuck himself tonight... and any other night, for that matter.

***

The next day, I wake up mid-morning, stretching my arms out. I think about when I left Rose's last night. I came straight home locked the door and pretended not to be home as Mark banged on the door. He was banging and yelling so loud, he woke up the neighbors. When Mr. Underwood, my neighbor, threatened to call the police, Mark left, but not before he yelled out some words to me about how my punishment would be given when he returned from his trip.

I think about how he punished me the last time I did something he didn't like, and my core starts to throb. The sex was out of this world. Who would have thought I would enjoy being tied down and spanked? I came harder than I ever have before. I never knew an orgasm could feel that good. I didn't think that was possible.

Jumping out of bed, I fix myself a quick bite to eat. I have a job interview in Cape Elizabeth, Maine, tomorrow. I plan on driving up today and staying the night.

The interview is at a small law firm, but it's precisely what I'm looking for. I've had a phone interview with human resources and will speak to the boss himself tomorrow. I'm over the moon excited.

CHAPTER THREE

Liz

My job interview was a success. They offered me the position before I left, and I accepted, knowing it was the right fit for me. The law firm and the town felt right.

When I left the law firm, I rode around the quaint town to find a place to rent. I found several apartments and a few homes, but one particular house stood out. It's a beautiful one-bedroom home with a big porch and swing. A white picket fence and gorgeous flower boxes enclose the small property. The best part of this quaint home is the ocean view across the street.

As I'm boxing up my things to move away from him and all the memories that I just want to forget, I can't help but remember. It hurts a little more than I thought it would. I don't start my new job for another two weeks, but I'm ready to leave and settle in my new place. I need peace of mind and a fresh start.

Wrapping the box with packaging tape to secure my belongings, I blow out a puff of air. Looking around the small apartment, I see the sad old furniture that came from a second-hand store. When I first moved in, I couldn't afford new furniture. Then, when I got money, I didn't bother replacing the ragged couch and recliner.

I'm not going to bother taking any furniture with me. I can easily replace it, which just makes moving lighter for me. Having only a handful of boxes will make it easier to fit into my car. I hear the doorbell ring, and I freeze. The fear of the visitor being Mark weighs heavily on my shoulders. I've known Mark to reschedule trips. His threat repeatedly replays in my mind, having me on edge.

Walking lightly to my front door, I peer out the door viewer and see Rose and Sarah's smiling faces.

Shit!

Glancing at the clock on the wall, I see it's after five. I've been so busy, I haven't even noticed the time. I stare back at the boxes I've stacked against the wall. I know they'll notice them.

Shit! Shit! Shit!

Another knock occurs.

"Liz," Rose yells out.

I open the door. "Hey, ladies!"

Rose walks in and stops. "Liz," she turns back to me. "What the fuck are you moving?"

"I'm—" I try to explain, but Rose cuts me off.

"Is it money? I can give you whatever you need," she says as she starts to look through the open box that's close to her.

Sarah just blinks back and forth.

Fuck!

I walk up to Rose and shut the lid to the open box. "Rose, I'm leaving New York."

The blood drains from her face, making her look pale.

"Listen, before you say anything, I have to tell you I've had my plans set into motion since before we became friends. This is something I've always wanted to do."

"Is this why you didn't take the position at Ross and

Archer?" Sarah asks.

"Yes, I've always wanted to get out of New York." I wait for Rose to say something, but she stands silent, her mouth opening and closing like a fish.

"Rose, just say it. I can tell you have something on the tip of your tongue."

"I don't know what to say. Does Mark know you're leaving?"

"Why would I need to tell him? He's just someone who works at Red." I try to hide the fact that we're fucking.

Rose tilts her head and raises an eyebrow. "We all know you two are fucking like you're in heat." She smiles.

Walking over to the couch, I fall back onto it, blowing air out of my cheeks.

"I can't believe everyone knows. I thought we were, or at least I was, doing a great job of hiding it. You know we're just fucking, nothing more."

I want more than just great sex.

They come over and sit down in the small living space.

"He's going to be pissed when he finds out you've left and didn't tell him," Sarah adds. "I wouldn't want to be on the receiving end of that." She widens her eyes for effect.

She's right. He will be pissed. I'll be taking his regular pussy from him.

"That's why you both,"—I point at them—"are not going to tell him or Wilder and Blaze. Right?" I wait for them to answer. I know it's asking a lot of them to keep quiet.

Rose holds her hand up as if she is about to pledge to a fraternity. "I promise I won't say anything unless Blaze asks. I can't lie to him. It's our code, no lying to each other," Rose says.

"Fine." I know their loyalty is to their men.

"Where are you moving to?" Sarah asks.

If they won't lie, then I don't want to share where I'm going.

"Upstate," I reply. Not telling them will give me the ability to leave without worrying if I will have time to get out of town.

They look at each other, and I can see their minds working. They're secretly telling each other they wouldn't want to be me.

I decide to change the subject because I'm tired of talking about Mark. Maybe he's found himself a new woman to boss around. He looked comfortable with the lady by his side at Rose's party.

There it is again. A sharpness in my chest—jealousy. I do my best to shake the feeling. It doesn't belong in my chest. Jealousy shouldn't hurt like it does, not over Mark.

***

I finished packing everything else when Rose and Sarah left yesterday. They wouldn't leave until I told them where I was going. I convinced them I would be okay and that I would call them when I arrived at my new place. They seemed to relax after they made me promise several times.

I load the last box in my car and head back up to my apartment.

When I walk in, I take in the lonely furniture and sad white walls. It's a bittersweet goodbye. This apartment was the first place I felt safe. A place where I didn't have to worry if my mother's boyfriends would do their best to take advantage of me. A place of my own in a safe neighborhood.

My cell pings in my back pocket, and I pull it out. It's a text from Rose.

Rose: I wanted to come see you before you left, but I'm unable to get away. I'm swamped with cases. Call or text me as soon as you get there. Then send me your new address. I mean it, Liz, don't walk out of my life. Love you!

Me: You have my word. Love you back!

I slide the phone back into my pocket and grab the last bag in the apartment. After taking one more look around, I shut the front door. Standing there facing it, I get lost in my thoughts.

I've just closed another chapter of my life. The thrill of closing this chapter should give me relief, but something is bubbling up from my stomach, making me feel uneasy.

CHAPTER FOUR

Mark

I walk into the basement of The Spot. The Spot is a nightclub in California that Wilder owns. The club brings in a lot of revenue, but it's also one of the biggest fucking headaches. That's the reason I had to come. As the hitchman, I take care of the fuckers who don't pay their loans.

The fact that I didn't eat Liz's sweet pussy before I had to leave is not helping my mood. I'm fucking pissed she didn't open the damn door before her fucking neighbor tried to call the police on me. If there hadn't been onlookers, he would have ended up in the East River.

Now standing in front of this piece of shit tied to the chair, I swing my arm and slam the hammer on his left hand. His bones crunch on impact. His screams are like music to my ears, except I wish they were Liz's screams when I ram my fat cock in her.

The punishment I plan on giving her when I get home will leave her remembering she's mine for days when she's not able to sit on that perfect ass.

The sorry son of a bitch not only doesn't pay his bills, but he beats his family. That's something I have a strong dislike for—men beating their wives and kids.

"Where's our money?" I stare at him intensely.

Wes Parker cries out as he intently watches for what tool I'll use next.

Fuck yes!

This shit never gets old. I love it when they cry, beg, and plead for their pathetic life. I tower over Wes with a sadistic smile. His shoulders hunch over, making him look like he's shrinking into his seat.

"Shall we go to the right hand, or shall I use these four-inch nails next?" I stare at Wes, but he doesn't bother looking up at me.

I nod to Crew. Crew and his twin brother, Drew, work with me to ensure we enforce the rules when you borrow money and don't want to pay it back.

Crew strolls over to Wes, yanking his hand flat to the table with two vice grips, one on his pointer and the second on his ring finger. Wes looks at his hand in panic. I laugh, and before he has time to make a decision. I slam the four-inch nail right between his pointer and middle finger, just grazing the knuckle by a hair, ensuring he won't be able to use it for a long time.

"Now, where is my money?"

"I... I don't have all of it," he sniffles like a fucking pussy. His face constricts in pain. I'm sure it's an agonizing feeling. I once had a car door shut on my hand, and it fucking hurt like a bitch.

Crew unties his hands, picks Wes up by the back of his shirt, and shoves him to the room entrance, making him trip over his own feet. He hits the side of his face against the doorframe, leaving a coat of red as he slides down to the floor.

There's just one more reminder I want to leave him with. I stomp over to Wes. Reaching down and grabbing him by the hair, I pull out my knife and hold it up to his face. When I release the blade, his eyes go wide.

"Never, ever think about hitting your wife or daughter again."

His eyes follow the blade as I lightly move it across his neck, right to left. When I reach his left ear, I flick the blade upward, severing his earlobe from his face. He screams, and I laugh maniacally, gesturing to Crew and Drew that Wes's time is up.

Crew and Drew pick him up and take him to collect what money we can get for now.

I wash my hands and head upstairs to grab a drink before leaving. When I sit at the bar, a long, skinny arm wraps around my neck.

"Mark, long time no see," Monica purrs. She looks me over.

I can feel how her eyes roam my form, likely calculating how she can get what she wants from me.

"Monica, how are things going with the new husband?" I almost laugh.

I've known Monica for years, and she is definitely not marriage material. She was the first woman I fucked when I started working at The Spot. Her pussy doesn't hold my interest anymore, not since I met Liz and took her virginity. Hmm, just thinking about Liz's sweet tight pussy makes my blood rush to the head of my cock. The fact I'm the only one who has had the great pleasure of hearing Liz scream from an orgasm sends pride straight to my black heart.

M'Aingeal. She's the only woman that I've ever been loyal to.

"It didn't last. He… wasn't you," she runs her hand from my shoulder down to my chest.

This time, I do laugh. I know my cock wasn't the only one she was sucking while I was fucking her.

I grab her hand before she can reach my dick.

"What's wrong? You know I can suck your cock like no one else can."

My dick doesn't even move. I might be a cold-hearted mother fucker, but Liz has the only pussy that can hold my dick prisoner. My cock would love nothing more than to be put in solitary confinement in that pretty little pink pussy every night.

I come from a family where respecting and being loyal to your woman is essential. Respect for women was an order from my dad. It was one of the few things we agreed on.

Where most men in my line of work have had shitty upbringings, mine was the opposite. My parents were and are still, to this day, happily married. They provided a substantial home for me and my much younger four sisters.

My dad is a fourth-generation brewmaster. He wanted to hand over our family brewery to me. Past tense, wanted to.

Everything changed when he figured out that I was the one who cut the brakes to his friend's, John Hallmark's, car. Just to say his name puts a sour taste in my mouth.

The fucker and his nitwit son came to our brewery one day. When my dad walked away, I overheard John talking to his son about sabotaging our brewery so he could drive our business to the ground.

So naturally, I didn't waste time cutting the brakes on their car. They crashed, but unfortunately, it didn't kill them.

When my dad saw the oil spill on the pavement in our parking lot after they left, he looked at me with knowing eyes. He knew I did something that he wasn't going to like. When the call came in that John and his dumbarse son had a wreck and it left his son paralyzed, my father lashed out and told me to leave. He wouldn't even hear me out, to let me tell him what I heard. He said for me to leave until I found a way to renew my devil ways, not to bother coming back.

I should have known better. Dad doesn't like how I handle business. Instead of taking the higher road, I take the bull by the balls and shove them so far up their arse that people know not to fuck me over.

My ways is what landed me this job with Wilder. He had heard of my reputation and called me to come work for him. He offered me enough money to make it worth the move.

John Hallmark doesn't know that it was me who cut his brakes. I imagine my dad never told him. He just wants to keep the peace between the two largest breweries in Ireland.

If only he knew.

"Not interested, sweetheart." I drop her hand away from my non-responsive cock.

She leans into me, her oversized silicone breasts brushing my shoulder. "I bet you I could ride your dick raw." She blows into my ear.

Fuck, her breath smells like she smoked a pack of cigarettes. It would make any man's dick shrivel up and hide.

Why had I never noticed that before?

I turn to look her in the face. Her eyes are dilated, and she's completely off balance. I grow a little concerned; maybe someone has put something in her drink.

"Monica, who are you here with?"

She doesn't respond. Her eyes roll to the back of her head, and she collapses.

Fuck!

CHAPTER FIVE

Liz

Darkness fills the air the farther north I drive, leaving blue skies behind me. The presence of a black cloud has clung to me ever since I left New York. I can't understand why I'm feeling this way when I should be experiencing the adrenaline rushing through my veins in excitement with my new life in motion.

I pull my car into the parking spot in front of the grocery store and pick up my purse. I'm not too far from my new house and want to gather a few groceries until I can make an official grocery run.

When I start to slide out of my car, I spot two broad men standing at the edge of the building, a haze of cigar smoke surrounding them. A set of unwanted eyes watch me from the lingering shadows. He blows out smoke from the corner of a rising smirk. I feel my pulse race and my body shiver.

Both men have wickedness that swirls around them, leaving destruction in their wake.

One of the men blows out the last of his inhaled nicotine, speaking to his friend without taking his eyes off me.

The second man looks up, and I almost lose what little food I have in my stomach. He looks too much like my mother's boyfriend from years ago. The boyfriend who almost raped me. If I hadn't gotten out of his grasp, I know he would have succeeded. There was no one around to help me. My worthless mother was out cold on the floor. Even if she weren't, she wouldn't have cared enough to stop him. She didn't give a damn about me.

My legs and hands are shaky. Taking a chance to stand on wobbly legs, I push open the car door. Placing one foot on the black asphalt, I rise to my feet and close my car door, ensuring the car is locked.

I peer up out from under the thick lashes that I inherited from my mother and look at the men. They are moving slowly in my direction. I walk in great strides toward the grocery store's door.

If I just get inside, I'll be safe.

When I make it inside, I almost run to the customer service desk. When I see the clerk, I do my best to speak without breaking down in tears.

"Can you help me?" I turn back, expecting to see the mysterious men, but they're nowhere to be seen.

I must be going out of my mind. There is no one here to hurt me, not here. I'm too far away from the sinfulness I left behind.

There is no need to act dramatically. I just simply need to grab a handful of things and head home.

"Where is your restroom?" Still feeling shaken up, I ask the young man who appears to be around my age, "Can you just show me? I'm new in town, and this is the first time I've been in here."

The man looks unhappy with my request, but he grabs his keys and opens the door to the office, locking it again when he shuts it behind us.

The entire time he escorts me, I keep my eyes set on my surroundings. The thought of being ambushed scares the shit out of me.

When we come to the doorway to the restrooms, I thank the gentleman for his help. "Thank you again for helping me."

"No problem. Can you find your way out?" He asks like a true smartass.

"It's a laborious task, but I imagine I can find my way out," I say sarcastically, giving him my best 'eat shit and choke on it' smile.

He laughs. "I'm Josh. If you need anything, just ask." He gives me a wink.

"Thanks, will do."

I finish up my personal business in the restroom and grab a cart to gather the handful of items to cook breakfast with.

Once I check out, I ask Mr. Split Personality if he will walk me out. There was no way I was going outside alone and running into those men without an eyewitness. If Josh came up missing, at least someone would be concerned enough to call the police. He's the manager, and the likelihood of one of his employees noticing he's gone is high.

Josh loads the last bag on my passenger side. "I'd like to get your number if you're willing to give it to a stranger." He looks almost shy asking me.

I smile. He's really cute, dark hair that has curls at the end, a thin, tall frame.

"Here," I pass my cell to him. "Enter your number, and I'll send you a text."

He takes it and enters his number, sending himself a text. "Now I have your number, and I plan on calling," he smirks.

"You don't even know my name." I'm a little shocked that he asked me out but didn't ask for my name.

"That's why I plan on calling to get to know you better."

Josh takes the cart, and I slide into my seat as he shuts my door. I give him a small wave bye. Starting my car, I leave the parking lot and head down the road.

The lights become dim as I head down the two-lane county road.

I'm the only car on the stretch of road until two headlights come up behind me at high speed, turning their bright lights on when they get mere inches from my bumper. I flip my rear mirror to dim the bright lights from blinding me.

Some people are just assholes!

"Go around me!" I scream at the car behind me.

The vehicle rides my bumper, then slacks off. The car sways behind me in the oncoming lane and back behind me, repeating the same pattern, trying to decide if they want to pass. I lower my window, throw my arm out, and motion for the car to pass me.

Nothing. The car still rides me, still swaying in and out of the lane. Trying to stay calm, I slow my car.

Maybe they will finally pass me.

The mystery vehicle pulls up beside me in the oncoming lane. I'm so frightened, I keep my gaze straight ahead, praying for a way out of this nightmare situation.

Without warning, the car jerks in my direction, sending my pulse to an unhealthy rate. I scream and pull the steering wheel to move in the opposite direction. My car skates across the graveled off-shoulder. I press my foot on the brake, almost stomping through the floorboard from the pressure I've applied.

My car comes to a halt while my tears stream down my cheeks, dripping onto my lap.

I blink, trying to dry them up. When I look around to grasp my bearings, I spot two red tail lights fading in the distance, as if I was a distant memory of their spiteful game.

CHAPTER SIX

Liz

It's been two weeks since my scare, the night someone ran me off the road. A part of me was worried it was someone from my past, but how could it be? I've moved away from anyone who I've known.

I never received a phone call or a text message from Josh, the man I met at the grocery store. It hasn't bothered me enough for me to return to his job to ask why.

Mark hasn't tried to contact me, which is what I wanted, but it hurts knowing that I was just a fuck for him.

When I close my eyes, I picture our last time together. How his rough hands spread between my shoulder blades, pressing me down onto the hard surface of the cold tile on the bathroom floor. He took his pleasure from me—hard—stealing small pieces of my broken heart in his conquest to possess my body.

Focus, Liz!

I shake my head, removing any thoughts of Mark. I need to forget about him and maybe try to date a good man. Someone I know doesn't come with danger warnings. Looking at my reflection in the sun visor, I apply a light shade of pink to my lips.

"This is the new start you wanted," I tell myself. "Then why am I not as excited as I should be?" I exhale.

I arrive early for my first day at Lawson Law. I want to make a good impression on my new boss, Mr. Lawson.

My nerves are getting the best of me today. I wasn't able to sleep last night. Something was gnawing at me all night. Every few minutes, I found myself returning to my front window, peering out, paranoid that someone was watching me.

Before leaving my car, I look around to scan my surroundings.

What am I looking for? No one knows where I am. No one but the two people who care about me the most, Rose and Sarah.

Opening my car, a breeze brushes my skin with the scent of salt water. I inhale a lung full of the fragrance through my nostrils. Serenity, the ocean air calms my nerves.

Lawson Law is only a twenty-minute drive from my house. The beautiful white column building looks as if it was once a family home. The white wood siding has age to it, leaving me wondering how old the building is.

I push open the front door to the law firm and step in front of the receptionist.

"Hi, I'm here to see Tom Lawson."

Tom is my new boss and also a partner in the law firm. He looks to be in his late thirties. His good looks resemble the men in The Kennedy family. His sandy blonde hair has unruly waves that spring across his face. His good looks could get him into any high-society event.

The young lady with purple hair looks up and asks, "Liz Black?"

"Yes."

"Have a seat. I'll let him know you're here."

Sitting down on the white wicker couch, I notice everything

looks white and crisp. It feels like I stepped into Cape Cod.

"Liz!" Mr. Lawson comes out of his office with a smile and sun-kissed skin, making his perfect large white teeth stand out.

"Did you meet Julie?" Mr. Lawson asks, pointing to the receptionist.

I keep my answer short, "We spoke," not wanting to go into detail that we didn't swap phone numbers.

"Julie will help you get any supplies you need. I will show you to your office and take you on a basic tour. Unfortunately, I'm tied up with meeting a client and have several conference calls this morning. Julie will also introduce you to the other staff members." Mr. Lawson leads me through the office as he continues to speak. "As you know, we only have thirty employees. We're nowhere near as large as Ross and Archer, but we're hoping you will enjoy it here just as much."

After Mr. Lawson spends all of ten minutes with me, he passes me off to Julie, who seems less than eager to help me.

Julie gets up from her desk, and I notice she's dressed in an outfit that came straight out of the eighties. Everything from the color of a bright orange blazer with the white shirt underneath to the matching bright orange knee shorts.

Yep, straight out of a Miami Vice scene.

Sadness washes over me when I think of how I wish Rose were here to see Julie's outfit. Rose has a love for bright colors.

"Can you follow me?" Julie asks while fanning her long nails around. "I'll show you where the office supply closet is."

We take a step in the opposite direction of Mr. Lawson's office, but before we can take the second step, the front door opens, and Benny Clarke steps into Lawson Law Firm.

Benny is the son of Jimmy Clark, the leader of the Irish Mafia. A real troublemaker. When Sarah and Wilder were at the beginning of their relationship, Benny caused real trouble. Wilder wanted to dispose of him, but luck was on Benny's side because of who his father is. It's the only reason he is still breathing today.

I freeze, silently praying to bleed into the hardwood floors. Maybe Benny won't recognize me. However, luck has never been in my favor.

Benny buttons his suit just as his eyes trail down my body. His crooked grin sends unwanted shivers up my spine, leaving an unpleasant taste in my mouth.

He sways over, letting his eyes roam my face.

"Miss Liz." He clicks his tongue. "You're looking like a dream."

Why is he here? What business could he possibly be doing in Maine?

Julie clears her throat. "Mr. Clarke, Mr. Lawson will be with you shortly."

Benny doesn't make a move to speak or to blink. We continue staring at each other until I speak.

"Mr. Clarke, thank you. You… look…" I can't bring myself to say well, no matter how good-looking he is. "Alive." I hold my breath.

Fuck, I didn't mean to say that. It slipped out.

He laughs. That laugh makes me want to run. Run until my legs give out. Until I run so far, I'm surrounded by no one or anything that could ever be from my past. No one to remind me of what I've had to overcome to get myself to this stage in my life.

"I should hope so," Benny remarks.

Mr. Lawson emerges from his office, and a frown appears on his features when he spots me talking to Benny.

Maybe he's not a fan of Benny's, like the rest of the world.

Mr. Lawson approaches us with a frown still in place on his face.

"Mr. Clarke."

Benny turns with a smile, reaching out to shake his hand.

"Mr. Lawson, good to see you again. Shall we go to your office to discuss business?"

My mouth gapes as I watch them walk into Mr. Lawson's office, and when the door shuts, I feel Julie's bony fingers on my shoulder tapping away.

"Hmm, Liz."

"Oh, sorry. I apologize."

Julie cocks her head. "Yeah, I hate to bring bad news, but I wouldn't look at that one with wanting eyes. He's not the type of man to settle for one woman. If you know what I mean." She motions for me to follow her.

Fuck, if she only knew.

CHAPTER SEVEN

Mark

Fuck!

Monica is lying on the floor as people stumble around her. I roll my eyes, forcing myself to get off the comfortable barstool.

This is not how I wanted my night to go. I was looking forward to getting balloobas, then stumbling my way back to my room. Take a hot, steamy shower and rub one out to the image in my mind of Liz's sweet little pussy.

When I get back to New York, I plan on punishing her for ignoring my demand to be at Red, wet and naked, waiting for me.

I scoop Monica up and take her to the office. I don't know if she drank too much or if she had something slipped into her drink. I don't really give a fuck, but I don't trust any of these arseholes not to touch an unconscious woman.

When I walk into the office, I push the door closed with my foot and lay Monica down on the black leather couch.

The office at The Spot isn't huge, just big enough to do bookwork. We perform most of the pleasurable work in the basement, where screams won't be heard.

As I rise, I feel hands sliding up to the zipper of my Armani pants.

"What the fuck!"

Monica's slitted eyes open, and her Botox lips form a smile. I grab her hands, squeezing them.

She winces.

Getting into her face, I spit out, "Tell me." My chest heaves. "Did you fake passing out?" Fire breathes through my nostrils, daring her to lie to me. Nothing pisses me off more than wasting my time. Especially on a woman I have no desire to fuck.

Monica tries to pull her hands out of my grip, but I don't give her any slack.

"I just thought—"

Cutting her off, my voice booms, "No, you didn't think." I look at her, at the smugness on her face. It disgusts me.

"I just wanted to be alone with you. I can make it up to you… on my knees?" She gives me a seductive look.

My lip curls up in a sneer. The last thing I want is my cock in her filthy mouth.

The door opens, and Crew walks in with his back to us. "Parker paid up." When he turns, his eyes trail down Monica's barely covered body. A smirk displays on his lips, and he hums in appreciation. I can't say Monica is ugly. Just not the right pussy for me.

My eyes move from Crew to Monica. She is no longer moving away from me but more drawn to me, as if she wants my protection. She's looking in the wrong place for protection.

I put her hands down and rise, but she grabs my shirt, bunching it up in her hands.

"Please don't… don't leave me with him," she begs.

Everyone knows Crew is the most sadistic when hurting women for pleasure. Of the Anderson twins, he is the most dangerous.

Blaze and I have had to cover up his fuck ups more than

once. He gets sick pleasure out of hurting women when he fucks them. That's the reason we watch him around the girls at Red. We don't want any of the ladies to come up dead.

I push her hands off me. Looking at Crew, I give him a nod to do what he wants. Monica should have thought twice about her little fucking act before she pulled it off.

When I leave, I head straight for the door. Drew is leaning against the outer wall close to the door, looking bored as shit.

"What the hell are you doing?" I ask.

He lets out a breath of air and looks around. "Where's Crew?"

"He'll be busy for a while."

"Fucking arse," Drew looks up at the ceiling.

Drew knows his twin brother better than anyone. He knows he'll need to be around to clean-up Crew's mess.

"I'm heading back to my room. Call me if you need help."

***

A day later, we arrive back in New York late. I jump into my Audi R8 and head straight to Red.

Liz should be at work, and I've had a hard-on ever since I woke up this morning. It took me jerking off twice to an image of Liz's tight pussy to fall asleep last night.

I walk into Red through the back door and head straight to Liz's room. The same room we've been fucking in for years.

Damn, I'm so fucking hard!

When I open the door, it's not Liz lying naked on the bed.

"Who the fuck are you?" I yell.

The small framed girl with barely any tits scoots back against the bed's headboard.

"I'm Jacqueline."

I storm out the door, grab my cell from my pocket, and dial Liz's number. She doesn't pick up, which isn't really a surprise. She knows she's due for her punishment, and I'm always good at my word.

When I march across the floor, looking like I'm about to murder someone, Blaze yells out to me from the bar.

"You look like someone stole your best friend," he laughs.

Mother fucker!

"What the fuck are you laughing at?" I glare at him.

"Fuck, man, don't be so serious. What the hell is wrong with you?"

Huffing I sit on a barstool next to Blaze and, order a whiskey. When the bartender sets it down in front of me, I throw it back, swallowing the contents in one gulp.

"Fuck, man, are you going to tell me who spit in your cheerios this morning, or should I not give a fuck?"

I take a breath and do my best to sound like I don't give a shit, and it doesn't bother me that Liz is gone. I don't want to sound like a weak pussy.

"I didn't see Liz come in," I say nonchalantly.

Blaze doesn't say a word, but when I turn to him, he has a fucking grin on his face that I would love to knock off.

"Yep, I knew that's why you were upset. I just wanted to fuck with you."

"Fucking arse," I murmur. "Where the fuck is she?"

"Don't know, but she hasn't been here for two weeks," Blaze announces.

I stand up, ready to drive over to her apartment, but Blaze stops me.

"Don't bother going to her apartment. It's completely empty. She doesn't live there anymore, and there's no forwarding address. I already checked when she didn't come in the first night."

My fury makes me snap, "Then why in the fuck have you not asked Rose?" I yell.

Blaze shrugs his shoulders. "Didn't think anything of it.

Lots of girls leave, but I didn't realize you two were more than fuck buddies. You don't get close to anyone."

He's right, I don't. I usually don't give a damn about any woman, but Liz is different. She's mine.

Mine from the beginning, from the moment I saw her with Candy. I knew I wanted her, but I didn't know she would put her mark on me, mark her ownership on my soul.

When I fucked Liz and I broke through that tight little pink pussy, her virgin blood marked my dick, claiming me.

When I took her virtue, there was a voidness in her eyes. She was detaching herself from me from that moment. After finding my release, she went to the bathroom and locked the door. I heard her cries through the thin walls, tugging at my cold, icy heart. Her tears cracked the frozen surface. When she came out of the bathroom, I tugged her down to the bed and held her close until we both fell asleep.

I'll stop at nothing to bring her back to where she belongs, back to my bed. Of course, when I get my hands on her, that punishment I promised will be warranted.

CHAPTER EIGHT

Liz

It's been two days since Benny Clarke stopped by Lawson Law, but his manic laugh still plays in my mind on repeat, still shakes me to my core, sending chills down my spine. It's a laugh I will never forget and one I pray I never hear again.

My friend Annie worked at Red for a short period of time. She ended up quitting because she felt unsafe. She never told me why.

After she left Red, she started working at a high-end restaurant. That's where she ended up meeting that piece of shit, Benny. He beat the shit out of her for not wanting to suck his dick in public for bragging rights, and that was the very first time I heard his spine-chilling laugh.

Love at first sight, she said.

Love. It's not a word that I've actually had the pleasure of knowing. I suppose my grandmother loved me, she was the only one.

Benny doesn't love anyone but himself. He beat Annie so severely, it took months for her face to heal, but the emotional damage was too significant.

She committed suicide, leaving a note explaining that she

felt like a failure and how everyone was better off without her.

There's a light knock on my office door, and Julie peeks her head through.

"Liz, would you like to go out for lunch today?"

Julie has warmed up to me. She's witty and apparently has to get to know someone before she talks to them. She walks in, setting some files on my desk.

"There's a great new Chinese restaurant with the best egg rolls!" Julie talks animatedly with her hands.

"Sounds good. Give me a few minutes to finish with my notes, and I'll be right out."

She smiles and walks out, leaving behind her files.

I'll take them to her when I head out.

I finish up my notes, grab my purse, and pick up the files. When the top file plunges to the floor and the contents scatter on the floor, I catch sight of Benny's name.

Curiosity gets the best of me. I bend down to pick up the papers that have spread across the floor. The name in bold print at the top of the document catches my eye. Benny Clarke. I try to quickly scan the documents, only getting a small glimpse of what looks like land being purchase by Benny before Julie comes back into my office, and I quickly start picking up the other papers, hoping she didn't notice what I was doing.

"Sorry," she says while helping me pick up the papers. "I got a little carried away talking and forgot Mr. Lawson's files."

"It's okay, I was bringing them to you."

After we get all the papers together, we head out for lunch. There's a small group of coworkers who take lunch every day together, and I guess I've been initiated into their group.

Julie and I sit together on one side of the booth while Ron and Bea sit across from us. We sit silently and watch the banter between the other two. I could be wrong, but I think Ron and Bea are fucking. No. They are fucking. They're sitting so close Bea is pressed up against Ron with not enough room to squeeze a feather between them.

While they fuss over what the office's air conditioning should be, I lean a little closer to Julie and try to talk low enough that Ron and Bea won't hear me.

"Does Mr. Lawson see Mr. Clarke often?"

Try to be discreet. Don't sound too eager.

Julie shrugs. "I'm not allowed to talk about Mr. Lawson's cases."

"Oh."

Fuck!

"I just know Benny Clarke is not the marrying type. My friend Lauren dated him, and he used her. Dropped her like a hot potato. That was when he first started coming to Lawson Law. She was so embarrassed about how she fell down the steps at his beach house. Got bruised up pretty bad. She quit shortly after that."

For fucks sake! I bet she fell down the steps.

"Where is she now?"

Dead?

"Don't know. I haven't heard from her, and she wouldn't tell anyone where she moved to. She just showed up one day, cleaned out her desk, and told me goodbye," Julie says between chewing her food.

Sound familiar, Liz?

After lunch, things are slow for the rest of the day until a distraught woman walks in twenty minutes before five.

Julie buzzes me. "Liz, there's a lady here asking to speak to someone for advice."

"Just show her in," I retort.

Julie escorts the lady to my office, where I wait for her. When she walks in, the woman looks as if she fell down about ten flights of stairs. I'm surprised she's able to walk at all.

I stand and welcome her to sit. "Please take a seat."

She shivers with fear. When she sits, I ask Julie to close the door for privacy.

"How can I help you?" I ask, looking over how badly bruised she is.

"I want to file for a divorce, but I don't have any money."

I already know the answer, but I still need to ask her the question. "Is your husband the cause of all your bruising?"

She looks at her shoes and nods her head, afraid to look me in the eye because she's ashamed of letting this happen to her. As if she blames herself, but truly, she's not the one to blame. It's the asshole who gets off on beating up a woman to make himself feel superior.

She's a prime example of why I wanted to go into law. I wanted to help women and their children who feel they are stuck in a situation and that there is no way out.

Also, the past struggles I went through with my mother. If someone—anyone—would have reached out to her and helped her, maybe she could have been a better mother, or maybe she was just too far deep in drugs to be helped. Regardless, those days are behind me, and now it's my time to help others.

"I can't guarantee anything because I'm new, but let me talk to my boss and see about doing your case pro bono."

She lifts her head and tries to smile, but the pain from the bruises makes her wince.

Handing her some forms, I ask her to fill them out, then I take notes on the many beatings she has endured during the short time she's been married. Two years and she's suffered more broken bones than a professional stuntman. I take photos for evidence, then we finish all the paperwork needed to get the ball rolling. When we finish, it's six thirty, and we're the last ones in the office.

I escort Mrs. Adams out and lock the door behind her when I hear Mr. Lawson in his office.

"Yes, I know. I'll have the papers drawn up and sent over for you to sign," he pauses. "Mr. Clarke, I assure you everything is in order."

When he hangs the phone up with a thump I tiptoe back to my office and gather my belongings, hoping he doesn't hear me when I leave.

***

It's been a busy first week in my new position as an assistant attorney. I'm finally feeling more relaxed and in more control of my life. When I pass the bar, I will be a full attorney. Excitement fills me, thinking I'm finally coming out of the darkness that has clouded my life. I'm finally feeling more relaxed and in more control of my life.

It's Friday night, and I'm home making homemade pizza out of pita bread. While the pizza is cooking, I give Rose a call. I've been missing her like crazy. She picks up on the first ring.

"Liz!" She screams into the phone. "How are you? Tell me about your new place and job."

I laugh. When Rose is really excited, she speaks so fast, it's hard to keep up.

"Everything is wonderful," I smile into the phone. "I have been missing our long talks during lunch. How are things with you and Blaze?"

"We're great! The sex is wonderful!"

"Rose!" I roll my eyes. "I don't need to hear about your sex life."

"Well, in case you wanted to know, I don't mind sharing. Talking about sex... have you had any lately?"

I inhale a lung full of air. "No. Let's talk about something else."

"Alright. Have you heard from Mark? He really flew off the handle when he got back, and you were gone. Called me,

54

demanding I tell him where you were. Of course, I didn't, but then he made Blaze ask me. I tried not to tell him, but he wouldn't let me have any orgasms during sex, and I broke down and told him." She pauses, "I'm sorry." She says in a small voice.

I knew it was coming. I knew Mark would find out, but hopefully, he's forgotten about me. Maybe he's moved on. Probably fucking the woman he was with at the party.

Grabbing my pita bread pizza, I walk out of the kitchen but stop in my tracks and scream at the top of my lungs, dropping everything in my hand.

There's a figure standing at my front window with something shining in his hand.

"Liz, Liz, what's wrong!" Rose is yelling from the phone that is lying on the floor.

I'm barely able to move standing frozen flash backs of my car being run off the road, the guy who asked for my number but hasn't called, seeing Benny here, could this be connected?

I fall to my knees as my eyes flood with tears. Silently hoping everything is just a coincidence.

CHAPTER NINE

Mark

Having Liz in my bed couldn't come soon enough. I waited a day too long for Rose to give Blaze Liz's whereabouts. No matter what type of look I gave Rose or how I threatened her, she wouldn't crack. So I had to rely on Blaze and his methods, whatever they were, to get the information out of Rose. I left the city the day Blaze gave me Liz's new address.

I arrived late last night and stayed in a hotel until this morning. Now, I'm standing across the street, watching her enter her car and drive out of my sight.

When she's gone, I walk across the street and pull out my pocketknife, popping the front door lock. Fuck, that was too easy. Anyone could get into this shitty house.

I close the front door behind me, instantly catching the scent I've missed. The hints of vanilla and lavender linger in the air, and my cock gets semi-hard. Fuck. The smell of Liz's shampoo finds me in my dreams, waking me up in the middle of the night with a hard dick that could drive holes through concrete blocks. I walk down the small hall that leads to the bedrooms.

When I enter Liz's bedroom, I see a pair of lace panties lying on the floor next to some clothes. When I pick them up, I bring them to my nose, close my eyes, and inhale.

"Hmm," I moan into the small material.

The scent of Liz's pussy goes straight to my dick. I do what any red-blooded man does. Unzipping my pants, I rub her lace underwear up and down my shaft. I close my eyes, and imagine her bouncing on my hard cock while flicking and sucking her hard nipples in my mouth. Listening to her sweet whimpers while I thrust inside her over and over again.

I feel that familiar tingle at the base of my spine, balls drawing up, and ropes of cum jet onto the thin material, my orgasm hitting me like a fucking train.

"Fuck!" I growl.

My breaths come out in great heaves. I've missed the scent of her pussy. She's the only woman who can make me cum that hard.

When I finally catch my breath, I tuck my dick back into my pants and walk over to Liz's pillow. The feather pillow is soft as I smear the cum filled lace panties onto the satin pillowcase.

I want her to smell my cum. I want her face to be covered in it. Maybe she'll dream of me when she inhales my scent.

***

The rest of the day, I stalk Liz, watching her from any corner that can hide my gigantic frame.

At the end of the workday, I notice Liz doesn't come out, so I wait for her, but I see I'm not the only one outside, surveilling the building.

There's a man in an old, piece-of-a-shit blue car parked in the lot, watching the law firm ever since a battered woman went in.

Alarms go off in my head as I watch this guy. So, I sit and wait to see what his plans are. When I see Liz open the front door, I sit straight up, ready to drive over the mother fucker if he tries to harm her.

Fuck, Liz has on a pencil skirt with a silk blouse. She looks every bit like a lawyer. Her skirt displays just how high and tight her arse is. I used to bite that arse every chance I got, and I plan on my teeth sinking into her delectable arse again—very soon.

A woman pops out behind Liz, and they shake hands. It's the same battered woman who walked into the firm earlier.

The ugly mother fucker in the blue piece of shit slumps in his seat.

Huh, hiding from someone, are we?

I go to work on following the fucker, writing down his tag number, and sending it to Blaze to pull any information he can.

I'm unsure if he's staking out Liz or her visitor, but I'm not losing my chance to find out what he's up to. If he's thinking of hurting *M'Aingeal*, he's not going to like the consequences of even thinking about hurting what's mine.

I follow the fucker to an older house. It's nice, not really my style, but I can't imagine he's pulling in much money. If he was, he should get a new car. The one he's driving is a fucking time bomb waiting to burst into flames.

Parking up the street, I watch him stagger up the front steps. He tries to open the door, but it's locked. When he pulls out a set of keys, he gets pissed. Banging on the door, the curtain opens, and the battered woman yells something out to him. They bicker back and front until the cops show up.

I leave after I watch them load him into the back of a patrol car. The fucker had to be hog-tied.

When darkness sets in, I stand outside of Liz's new house. Carefully popping the lock, I drift into her safety nest. I can hear her light snores down the hallway. As I draw closer to her bedroom, I think of how this place is completely unsafe for a single woman to be living in. Too easy to break into.

A dark shadow reflects onto the floor, moving in the same direction as I do. For the first time, I see how my dad sees me—an evil phantom that lurks around, stealing lives.

A hint of sadness races across my mind as I think about how he thinks of me, but in an instant, it's gone. There are no regrets about how I live my life, or how I conduct business. No regrets in taking lives—lives that are better off dead than living.

When I stand to the side of Liz's bed, I soak in the beauty of my woman as she's spread out. I can't help but want to devour her.

I smirk when I see she has the side of her face-planted into her pillow. The same pillow I wiped my cum on.

I would love to take my dick out and cum all over her pretty lips, but that can wait for another night. I watch her sleep for a couple of hours, ensuring she is safe here. I kiss her forehead before leaving the same way I entered and making my way back to my hotel.

The next couple of days, I stalk Liz, and each night, I let myself in her house to watch her. My favorite time is watching her sleep. The way she spreads herself out with one leg out of the covers makes me realize she's unaware of the danger that's in her bedroom each night.

It's late at night, and I'm watching Liz's house from across the street. I see movement out of the corner of my eye, and it's coming from the bushes. It's then I realize it's a man.

Grabbing my gun, I jump out of my car. I run to the bush, but before I get to the man, I hear a scream. My heart races out of control. I know who that scream belongs to. It's Liz.

She spotted him before I could get there in time. Quickly running up to him, I yank him back and smash him in the face with the side of my gun, knocking him out and dragging him out of the yard. I use my remote and pop the hatch to the trunk of my car. Picking him up, I throw his arse into my trunk. I jump into the car and ride down the road, instantly regretting not comforting Liz.

I can't believe this fucker would show up at Liz's house.

CHAPTER TEN

Mark

The stupid fucker is kicking and hitting the inside of the trunk of my rental car. I pull up to a remote section of the beach and get out, popping the truck. When the man slithers out of the trunk, I jerk him down to the ground.

It's the man from the law firm. The one who was watching Liz and the battered woman.

"What the fuck are you doing at my woman's house?" I tower over the man while he scrambles to get up.

When he finally stands up, he sneers, "Maybe you should keep that bitch in her place—the kitchen."

I don't speak. This fucker just gets off on words. I walk around the car and pull out my tongue teaser. I will pull his tongue out for calling *M'Aingeal* a bitch. When he sees me coming with the metal device in my hand, he starts to take off.

Figures.

Pulling my knife out of my ankle holster, I throw it, and it stabs the fucker right between the shoulder blades. He goes down, landing on the sand with a thump.

Strolling over to him, I pick him up by the hair and look at my watch. Tonight, I had planned on making my presence known to Liz and being balls deep inside of her.

Cutting this guy's throat wouldn't be good enough. I pull out my knife, twisting it, making sure this idiot feels more pain. He arches his back as he screams from the pain I carve in his back. He's paralyzed from the pain. As I drag his arse back to my car, I throw him back into it.

Making the decision that will benefit his wife's life, I plan to take his life tonight. He doesn't deserve to live.

***

Once I've finished snuffing out another life, I head back to Liz's. It's two in the morning when I let myself into her house.

Standing in the same spot where I've stood for the past few nights, I stare at long, lean legs that have kicked the covers aside. Liz's little pink panties with a bow are on full display. I want to wrap those gorgeous legs around my head as she cums all over my face.

Slowly, I move the covers out of my way. Lying down next to her, I grab my pocketknife, flicking it open. Reaching down, I slowly trail the blade from her calf all the way up to her thigh. Suddenly, her eyes fly open, and she gasps when she sees me.

"*M'Aingeal*," I say darkly, pressing the blade to the delicate skin of her throat with one hand and covering her mouth with the other. "You've been a bad girl. You knew I was going to come for you. You're mine, Lizzie... mine. I'll never let you go. Since you decided to do something stupid, I'm going to punish you, so you'll never forget who you truly belong to."

She mumbles unintelligible words, but I don't give a fuck.

Smirking, I slide the blade down the front of her tight camisole, cutting it right down the middle. She's not going to need that anymore. The moonlight shining through the window illuminates her perfect body. Her nipples pebble as

62

soon as the cool air hits them, and I can't wait to have a taste. I have to be patient. She's taken two weeks from me, so I have to take my time.

"Tell me, *M'Aingeal,* have you missed my cock?" I ask, arching a brow at her in question.

"I-I..." she stutters, but I feel her body shiver.

"Don't fucking move. If you get up, this punishment will be even worse." I don't give her time to answer. I want her to fuck up because when she does, the punishment will be even worse.

Sliding off the bed, I stand up and move down to grasp her legs. Wrapping my large hands around her ankles, I roughly pull her down the bed. Her perfect tits are clearly on display for me. I can't control my desire for her. My cock is already dripping precum. I can't wait to bury my cock deep inside *M'Aingeal's* tight pink pussy. It's been far too long without her.

I lean over her body, anxious to play. My fingers spread around her breast, and I pull it into my mouth, sucking and licking her nipple while pinching and pulling the other one between my fingers. I hum as my tongue circles her pebbled nipple.

I hear Liz suck in a deep breath of air, and her hips thrust up. Yeah, I bet she's so fucking wet for me. I give her nipple one last long, slow lick before backing away.

"Tell me, have you let anyone touch your pussy?" I reach for my knife again, and with the flick of my wrist, both sides of her lace panties are destroyed.

When she doesn't answer, I circle her clit with the tip of the blade, slightly nicking the delicate skin. Small rivulets of blood trickle down her already glistening pussy.

"Don't fucking lie to me."

Her back arches, her eyes close, and she begs for more pressure on her clit. My girl likes a little bit of pain with her pleasure, but I'm not going to give it to her. She's been a bad girl and needs to be punished, but first, I need to know if she's allowed anyone else to touch what's mine.

"No, no, I haven't been with anyone," she says breathily.

She better be fucking glad that no man has gone near what's mine. If anyone did, they would be a dead son of a bitch.

Lowering myself between her thighs, I take in the sweet scent of her pussy. It's been too long, and I just need a taste.

"Don't fucking move."

She whimpers, knowing that if she doesn't do what I say, I'll stop. I start nipping at her thighs. Her creamy pale skin is what dreams are made of. But when my marks are all over her skin, knowing I've claimed her like no other man has, my cock weeps.

One deep lick from her puckered hole up to her clit has her hips rising off the bed. I dive in like a man who's been starved for way too long, licking and sucking her clit. She tastes fucking divine, and the taste of her blood on my tongue makes me ravenous. Thrusting two fingers inside her tight pussy, I hit that sweet spot I know drives her crazy, keeping my mouth focused on her sweet little clit. Her breathing picks up, and I can feel her walls tightening around my fingers.

"Does that feel good, *M'Aingeal*?" All I get are those sweet moans that I love so much.

Slowly circling her clit, I move up her body, whispering in her ear, "Should I let you come, *M'Aingeal*?" She shivers in response. I bite down on her nipple and suck it deep into my mouth.

"Yes," she whimpering, begging me. "Please let me come." Her hips buckle forward.

Humming over her other nipple, I say, "No, you don't get to." Her mouth drops open in shock. "With your mouth open like that, I'm taking that as an invitation to shove my cock down your throat."

She closes it and swallows. I stop circling her clit and pull my hand back.

"What… what are you doing?" Liz asks, propping herself on her elbows.

Not answering her, I grab her and toss her on her stomach, unzipping my pants and letting my cock spring free. I am so damn hard right now. Precum continues to drip from my slit. Gripping my throbbing shaft, I give it a few tugs while I slap Liz on the arse with my free hand. She yelps and looks back at me.

"That's one for misbehaving." I slap her arse again.

Liz lets out another yelp. When she tries to put her hand over her round arse to stop what I'm doing, I push it aside, holding her hips and biting her arse hard. I've been imagining doing that for far too long. I can see my teeth prints and the trickle of blood falling down the curve of her skin, marking her as mine.

"Mark!" Liz screams.

Wrapping her hair around my hand, I yank her head back as I slam my cock into her tight wet pussy, causing her to moan out my name.

"Fuck! *M'Aingeal*, you're dripping for me."

I squeeze my eyes shut when she moans for me. My dick is so sensitive, I need a minute to keep from blowing my load too soon.

Liz's pretty pink pussy is the best pussy I've stuck my dick into. It's warm, soft, and tight—perfection. It's ruined any chance of another pussy having my cock inside it. Her pussy was made for me and me alone, but she doesn't know that.

I slam into her again, and she cries out in pleasure from the feeling of my fat cock stretching her, forcing her body to remember how to fit me. And it will—her body was made for my cock.

Pulling my cock out of her, I see her sweet juices running down her thighs. Spreading her arse cheeks wide, I spit, watching it leave a trail all the way down to that tight hole I'm about to fuck. I line myself up with her puckered hole, and she moans. My girl knows what's coming.

I've fucked her in the arse several times, but tonight I plan on fucking her hard. Hard enough for her to remember my promise of punishing her.

She will know she won't be able to run from me again.

When I push the head of my cock in, she turns her neck to look back at me. Her expressive eyes betray her. They have a way of showing me exactly how she's feeling. I can see the fear in them. She knows I'll punish her arse with my cock.

Pushing my dick in all the way, her hands fist the sheets.

"Oh, hell yes! This arse is so damn tight." I throw my head back, feeling her muscles tighten around my cock.

All my restraint comes loose, and my blood rushes to the head of my cock. I growl as I dig my fingers into her soft flesh, knowing there will be bruises tomorrow. Pulling out and thrusting back in at a punishing pace makes the old iron bed shake across the floor.

Leaning forward, I grab Liz's tits with both hands, squeezing them and tugging hard on both of her nipples. I fuck her arse hard enough that the shape of my cock will be branded inside of her for life.

Liz's moans grow louder with each punishing thrust. She arches her back, pushing her arse out, allowing me to get a deeper feeling. The sound of our skin slapping together echoes through the room.

"Please, Mark," Liz begs.

I know what she wants, but she doesn't get to come. Not tonight. Tonight, it's about showing her who she belongs to.

Letting go of one of her breasts, I grab her hair and pull her head back, taking her lips in a brutal kiss. Our breathing is in perfect sync with each other, just like our tongues.

When I break the kiss, I whisper to her, "After I fuck your

arse. I'll let you clean my cock with your mouth."

"Fuck you," she says bitterly.

"Isn't that what I'm doing now?" I laugh, shoving her down onto the bed as I thrust in and out of her tight arse.

"Fuck you," she says again.

I reach around to her pussy and slap it. She moans into the sheet. Her moans make my balls draw up. Spots dot my vision as I pull out of Liz. Grabbing my cock, I aim at Liz's arse, painting it with ropes and ropes of my cum.

"Fuck yes!" I scream as the last of my orgasm shoots onto her skin.

Falling onto Liz, our bodies slap together, and I don't give a shit when I feel my cum pressed into our skin.

"I've missed you, *M'Aingeal*," I whisper into her ear.

She doesn't say anything, but I guess I shouldn't have expected her to, but a small part of me had hoped she would.

I roll off her, lying on my back.

"Lizzie," I taunt her. "Clean me up with your tongue. Don't forget my sack, and don't leave a drop."

I'm a fucking arse, but it's why I'm so good at what I do.

CHAPTER ELEVEN

Liz

My eyelids are heavy as I lift them, only to close them against the blinding sunlight filling the room. I reach for the duvet to draw over my head but cannot grab it. That's when I noticed there's no cover on the bed. I'm lying in my bed completely naked with sticky thighs and a sore ass. WHAT. THE. FUCK.

The last thing I remember was passing out from exhaustion from Mark's appetite for endless sex. The man may be ten years older than me, but his stamina has always been high. He can fuck for hours and never get tired. The man is insatiable.

I hate that I love to be pleasured by Mark's cock, and I'm never able to deny him. My body craves his touch, his roughness. Everything that is him. His touch shocks my core. He takes from me, and I'm helpless when he does.

When I roll over onto my back, I wish I hadn't. The soreness in my ass is too painful. The pain shoots through me like a sharp knife.

"Oh God," I bellow.

Rolling back to my stomach, I feel instant relief.

"What's the matter?" Mark taunts. "Are you feeling the

effect of your punishment?"

Standing in the bedroom doorway, his broad chest drips small pearls of water off his muscular chest and abs, all the way down to his adonis belt. I hate myself for wanting to lick each drop off his beautiful body.

Fuck! I'm already wet again!

His near presence alone makes me want to get down on my knees and worship his cock like the dirty little slut I feel I am when I'm around him.

His handsome features, sinful body, and thick cock—no woman could deny him anything he would ask for.

I jump when his phone rings. Glancing over to the bedside table, the name Caoimhe is lit up on his caller ID.

Who is Caoimhe?

Mark walks over, looks at the screen, and answers, *"An bhfuil gach rud ceart go leor?"* (Is everything okay?)

He speaks softer than I usually hear him, and I can tell that whoever is on the line must be important to him.

"Tá mé ar mo bhealach," he hangs up the phone, then dials a number.

Speaking Gaelic into the phone, he looks at me, and I can sense a change in him. It's written on his face. His facial features set into hardness. When he ends his phone call, he doesn't speak as he walks inside my closet.

Scurrying out of bed, I quickly go to my closet, wondering what he's doing. I gasp when I see him yanking my clothes off the hangers.

"What the fuck are you doing with my clothes?" I grab his arm, trying to pull it away from my clothes, but it doesn't do any good. He's much larger and stronger than I am.

"You're leaving," Mark simply replies while he removes my clothes from the hangers. He pulls a suitcase from a shelf, opens it, and shoves my clothes in.

"I'm not leaving," I shout. "I'm not going anywhere."

Bending down, I pick up my clothes off the closet floor, trying to hang them back on the hangers. When Mark grabs my wrist, he gives it a squeeze.

My eyes meet his, and I see flames behind those beautiful *Amber Eyes* blazing, making them shine brighter. I can feel his anger burn my skin as his grip becomes tighter.

I try to pull my hand loose, but it does no good. With Mark, there is no escaping.

"You're going to do what I tell you to do. I'm not leaving you here. This house is crap, and anyone could break in," he says with a growl.

"I can get a security system. I'm not going with you." I say with firmness in my tone.

The side of his mouth moves up, and his eyes drift down to my breasts, where they linger briefly before they lower to my pussy.

I shrink into myself. I was so wrapped up in what he was doing I had forgotten about being completely naked.

I take a step back, but I can't get loose. I keep trying to pry his hand off my wrist. His smirk taunts me, leading me into a corner as his enormous frame engulfs me, making me feel small.

"I have the jet waiting for us. Gather your things up and get ready to leave." Darkness laces his words, making a shiver run down my spine.

Mark looks down at my full breasts, licking his lips. He places his hand over my breast, rolling my nipple between his fingers. I close my eyes, trying to hold back a moan as my arousal coats my inner thighs.

His breath rolls off my neck when his mouth lightly moves to my ear.

"Tell me." His hand moves to my hip, then around to my bare ass, giving it a hard squeeze. "Are you wet for me, Lizzie?"

I slap his hand away, and he laughs darkly.

"Get your stuff together. We're leaving in an hour."

Mark walks out, leaving me in a hot, wet state of hormones and conflicting feelings of wanting and hating him.

I know I won't be able to get away but I don't want to lose my job. I go to grab my cell phone off my nightstand and send a text to my boss letting him know that I need time off for a family emergency out of the country. He replies within seconds letting me know to take what time I need off and to keep him inform. Exhaling I walk over to my closet and grab a suitcase.

Once I pack my suitcase, there's a loud commotion in the living room—the sound of glass shattering rings in my ears. Fear sweeps over me, and I'm breathing heavily, unable to process what is happening.

Mark is yelling and cursing as I run into the living room. The large picture window that once gave me a beautiful clear ocean view now lies in sharp pieces of glass on the floor.

Mark draws his gun and runs to the front door as tires screech on the black asphalt in front of the house. The smoke left behind drifts into the house like a bad omen.

Gunfire erupts, and I immediately fall on the glass, cutting my hands and legs as I try to crawl my way out, begging myself to wake up from this nightmare.

Mark's voice gets louder as he yells, "Son of a fucking bitch!"

The sound of crunching glass gets closer, and two hands lift me up.

"Are you hurt?" Mark's eyes wander over me. He inspects the damage the broken glass has caused. "Fuck!" He says under his breath. "Do you have a first aid kit?"

"No, I don't."

"Shit!"

Mark lifts me up on the table, pulling his phone out and

grabbing a towel. He returns and pulls the small pieces of glass out of my legs and arms, carefully cleaning the blood from the scrapes.

"Did you get a look at who did this?" I ask.

"No, they had blacked-out windows."

There's a great deal of tension on his face, as if he's worried. Sliding my hand over his, which is currently cleaning my wounds, I ask, "What's wrong? I can tell it's more than just what happened."

Mark never gets shaken by anything. In all the blood baths that this cold, hardened man has been in, I've seen nothing that rattles him. Mark's eyes are cold. The amber fire that was in them a moment before extinguished.

"I need to head home, and you are coming with me."

"I'm not going back to New York." I protest.

Mark brings his nose to mine.

"I'm not going to New York. I'm going home to Cork, Ireland, and if I was going to New York, you wouldn't have a say, *M'Aingeal*. I own you. You. Are. Mine. You will go where I tell you to. Do you understand?"

Shivers rain down my spine as I nod in agreement. He's never been so fierce as he is now, and a desire to want him more pours into my broken heart.

I know it's wrong to want a man who is as dangerous as Mark, but now it's not just my body—it's my heart.

CHAPTER TWELVE

Mark

My eyes haven't left Liz the entire flight. If I didn't have a family emergency to attend to, I would have chased down the fucker who threw the brick through her window and killed them.

That's not the only thing they did. They hung a dead black cat in the doorway. When I threw the door open to chase the car, the corpse swung before me. I jerked it down, removing it before Liz could see it.

I can tell by the constant twisting in her seat and nibbling on her bottom lip that the disturbance is weighing heavily on her mind. When we return, I plan on hunting down the fucker and making their life miserable.

Liz meeting my family is not something I ever meant to happen. I enjoy the pleasure of a woman's body with no strings attached, but bringing any woman around to meet my parents or sisters has never been on the table for me.

I live in the shadows, seeking lives to steal. Living in a world filled with fucking flowers and white picket fences and normal fucking isn't for me.

I'm close to my mum and sisters because I've provided a

way for them to come to see me, but I've never wanted to go back home. Yet when my sister called me, crying about my father, I knew I had to.

We land in Cork, and I get the same proud feeling I once had to be home. Everything here is older, and our family heritage is written in everything we do and have.

Liz's eyes light up, taking in the scenery. I know she had a shitty life growing up. I pulled her records and took inventory of how she bounced from her grandmother to her mother, all the custody paperwork filled up with two folders. I can't imagine what she must have gone through as a child. It makes me more protective of her, knowing she had to endure such a shitty life.

"Go get our rental car," I tell Liz as we exit the plane, taking out my credit card. "Here, take this and DO. NOT try to escape." I lean in closer to her ear, nibbling on it. "You remember the pounding your arse took?"

Liz nods.

"I will surpass what I did last time." Making eye contact, I say, "Go be my good little girl and do what I ask." I reach around and slap her arse, sending her on her way.

Watching Liz sashay off stirs my need to fuck her. Liz does things to my dick I can't comprehend. Just her nearness drives me to insanity of want and lust.

Her breathtaking beauty is amplified by her hard outer shell. I want to peel back her outer layers to seep into her heart.

I hear a screeching noise, the sound that resembles nails against a chalkboard.

Looking around to find Liz, I see the side of the clerk, and it appears she is giving Liz shit.

When I walk over, I ask Liz, "What seems to be the problem?"

"She won't let me get a rental car with your card," Liz

replies, pointing to the clerk.

My head snaps to the clerk.

Fuck! Roxy.

Roxy was on my speed dial when I lived at home whenever I needed my cock sucked.

"Mark!" Roxy's face lit up, "I didn't know you were back," Roxy remarks, batting her fake eyelashes.

"Liz, take the luggage and meet me over there," I nod to the seats nearby.

When Liz sits, I look at Roxy and crack my neck. It's something I do when I speak to a woman sternly. It helps me to get the tension out, so I don't kill her.

"We need a rental car. Will you help us or act like a bitch to my woman?"

Roxy's face drops. She didn't expect me to have someone, and I can't blame her. I'm a fucking arse and don't deserve Liz.

***

Once I get the rental car taken care of, we finally get on the road. My parent's manor is about a thirty-minute drive from Cork. Liz has been silent since we left the rental place.

"What are you thinking?" I ask, breaking the silence.

She takes a deep inhale of air and releases it as if she is also holding some tension.

"Who was that woman?"

"Someone I used to know a long time ago. No one to be concerned with."

I pull the car into the driveway of O'Brian Manor and park.

"Where are we?"

"We're at my parents' manor." Getting out of the car, Liz grabs my hand.

"Are you fucking serious?" Her jaw drops. "Why the hell would you bring me here?"

"Because, *M'Aingeal*, I need my cock sucked more often, and your mouth pleases me. Now get your arse out of the car."

"Why don't you get your whore to suck you off?"

"Why would I get someone else when my cock fits perfectly in that sassy mouth of yours? Now, I won't say it again. GET. OUT. OF. THE. CAR."

Liz balls her fist up and grits her teeth, but like the good girl she is, she opens the car door.

My sister Grace, who's the baby in the family, opens the front door and runs to me with excitement on her beautiful face.

"Mark!" She jumps up, wrapping both arms around my neck and giving me a hard squeeze.

"Grace," I laugh. "Good to see you, too."

When Grace pulls back, she sees Liz as she exits the car. She grins, and I shake my head as if to say no, this isn't bringing my girlfriend home kind of trip.

Grace walks around the car. "Hi, I'm Grace. Mark's sister." She hugs Liz.

Liz pats her on the back and smiles at her, but it looks forced.

They're about the same age and frame, except Liz is more filled out than Grace. Grace had stomach issues when she was very young. We've been more than protective of her.

I grab our luggage and ask Grace where Mum is.

"She's with father in their room. You know he hasn't woken."

I nod. "Caoimhe has informed me."

As soon as we walk into the manor, I'm flooded with memories of my family—gathering with friends I grew up with, sneaking girls into my bedroom, and most precious of all, the memories of my parents and sisters gathering together to play games.

Liz looks around the manor, observing the age and

gracefulness of the Palladian-style façade. The manor sits on a hundred acres and has been in our family for centuries. Even as old as it is, our family has maintained it, and it is in good shape. Something I'm also proud of.

Mum walks down the grand entry staircase, looking as elegant as she always does. Her hair is pulled up in a bun, and she's wearing a fitted dress that falls slightly below her knees. She looks and always presents herself with elegance. Mum smiles, but it doesn't reach her eyes.

My parents were childhood sweethearts. They had me when they were too young, and my sisters came around the time when I was getting out of the single digits.

I cared for my sisters like a father as they grew up since my dad was always working. He wanted to grow the brewery business my grandfather started, and it called for long hours.

That's why I'm here now.

There was an explosion in the brewery. The electric wires caused a fire. That's what my family was told. My intuition says otherwise. I have a feeling someone started it on purpose.

The fact that it happened when my father was the only one in the factory is a little off to me.

"I'm so glad you came. He's still in a coma. Doctors said he was lucky to get out alive," Mum says as a tear escapes. She wipes the tear away. "And who is this?"

"This is Liz."

"It's a pleasure to have you, Liz." Mum pulls Liz in for a hug. "I know it was a long flight. You two freshen up, then we will have dinner."

Once we get settled, I go to my parent's bedroom to see my father. He's lying on the bed with cuts and burn marks on his hands and arms. He was lucky that's all he sustained.

CHAPTER THIRTEEN

Liz

Sitting in a dark room that's larger than my rental, I feel lost. Do I even know who Mark is? I thought his evil ways were clearly a product of his upbringing. I was wrong.

Looking around the large bedroom that's furnished more lavishly than Rose and Blaze's penthouse, I realize I don't know who he is at all. How did he become the man he is? His family is normal… above normal, really.

There's a small knock at the door, and Grace pops her head in.

"Would you like to go to town with me?"

"Very much."

Anything to get out of this house and put some distance between me and my devil.

"Let me know when you're ready. I'll be downstairs," Grace says.

I stand. "I just need to grab my bag." Walking over to the lounge chair, I pick it up. "Ready."

We walk out of the bedroom and make our way down the grand staircase. Mark is standing at the end of the staircase, his dark ambers fixed on me, watching every move my body makes.

"Where do you think you're going?" he asks when we reach the last step.

I glare at him through slitted eyes.

"We're going into town to shop," Grace replies, but Mark's eyes don't release me from their hold.

Grace reaches for my hand, but Mark grabs it first and tells her to step outside.

"What, can I not leave without your permission?" I ask through gritted teeth.

A sinister grin appears on his beautiful, smug face, and I want to slap it off.

"I won't take your back talk in front of my family. This is your first and last warning." He leans into my ear. "It would do you good to remember the punishment that happened to that beautiful plump arse of yours." His eyes light up. "Hmm, I'm fucking hard just thinking about it."

I push him aside, storming out of the house. I hear his laughter when I close the door.

Fucking asshole!

***

Grace and I have been shopping most of the morning. I haven't been purchasing, but Grace has bought more than enough for both of us. I had no idea someone could use that many clothes.

Standing outside the dressing room yet again, I tell Grace, "I'm going to walk over and grab a cup of coffee."

"Okay, I'll be over soon."

There's a small, cute coffee shop next door, and the smell of fresh beans being brewed keeps drifting in every time the shop door opens, making my mouth water.

I hand Grace's bags to her and walk out. The town is so beautiful. Bright colors are on so many buildings, making it so different from any place I've ever seen.

Walking into the coffee shop, I almost run over a man in a wheelchair.

"Sorry, I wasn't paying attention," I tell him.

"I think it was me. My cell distracted me," he says with a charming accent and a radiating smile.

I feel my cheeks flush. "Are you headed in?" Pointing to the coffee shop, I open the door for him.

"Depends. Are you heading in there?"

His charm is turned on high, but it feels wrong. Can a man truly be that charming and sincere? Maybe I'm not used to men being kind and not expecting anything in return.

"Yes."

"Do you mind if I join you?"

I offer him a tight-lipped smile. "Not at all."

If Grace comes over to the coffee shop and sees me with another man, Mark will find out. I'll go in, grab a cup of coffee and leave.

"Jacob Hallmark, and you are?"

"Liz Black."

"Please allow me to get the door, ma'am."

A large man steps out from behind Mr. Hallmark and opens the door, allowing me to enter first.

Something swirls in my stomach, making me feel uneasy. Once inside, I look out the windows to see if Mark is watching me, but there's no sign of him. Even knowing he's not around, I still don't feel relaxed.

Once we reach the counter, I order a black coffee, and Mr. Hallmark orders his latte.

"Thank you for the coffee, but I need to get going. My… friend will be looking for me."

"Please sit with me for a few minutes. I would love the company."

Hating to be rude, I sit at a table next to a large window, the only table available. I hope Grace doesn't come out and see me with another man.

"Mr. Hallmark, I really —"

"Please call me Jacob," he says with a devilish smile.

"Jacob."

"Are we on a first-name basis?" a deep voice asks.

I freeze, then shivers run throughout my body.

"Mark," I try to explain to him why I'm here with another man, but his hand comes up to halt me from speaking any further.

"Jacob, are you trying to take something away again that doesn't belong to you?" Mark asks in a strained voice.

Jacob laughs, and it's not the same laugh or smile he gave me.

"Mark, I didn't know she belonged to you. Maybe you would like to share like we used to?" Jacob smirks, taunting Mark.

My teeth grind in annoyance at the mention that Mark has had so many lovers. I hate feeling so jealous of the other women Mark has been with.

"Maybe I'll just give her to you when I'm done. You seem to like my leftovers," Mark remarks without emotion in his voice.

My stomach knots up, and I'm furious at how he thinks I'm his possession, yet he could toss me away whenever he feels like it. What the fuck am I to him? Just another fuck?

That's right, I'm just another fuck.

I throw my napkin down and stand.

"Thank you, Jacob, for the coffee, but I must be getting back to my friend."

I try to step around Mark to leave, but his hand catches my arm.

"Not yet. We have things to discuss."

Turning around to let him see the fire in my eyes and the

hate on my face for him, I twist my hand around until he lets
go.

"I think you have said enough. Now let the fuck go," I
whisper in a low voice. Heading to the door, leaving him
standing in the same spot, I feel the heat of his glare on my
back as I walk out.

I meet back up with Grace, and we finish the day with a
few more shops she wants to go through.

"How did you and my brother meet?" Grace asks me as we
walk along the sidewalk.

Fuck!

"We met at a club," I tell her, not mentioning that it's a club
where people go to fuck.

"You don't have to tell me. I know my brother is not into
legal things. He's always been the black sheep of our family.
My sisters and I have always known, even if our father tries
not to say anything."

"What does your dad say?" I ask, wanting to know more
about Mark's life.

"Nothing, really. He never mentions Mark, but I can tell he's
missed him the last few years. Our father is getting older, and
his ways are softening." She smiles at me. "I'm so glad he
brought you to meet us. He has never had a girlfriend, from
what I can remember. You must be important to him."

Yeah, like a dog and his bone. Chew on it for a while and bury it.

It's late when we return to the manor, and Mark is nowhere
in sight. Wanting to grab a hot shower and head to bed, I enter
the luxury bathroom and start the water.

The spray comes out strong in the two-head shower that's
big enough to fit a family. I let my pants slide down to a pool
at my feet and push my panties down. When I enter the
shower, the water hits my skin, and all the tension releases…
until my devil steps in behind me.

CHAPTER FOURTEEN

Mark

Walking into the steamy bathroom, I pull my t-shirt over my head and slide down my jeans before stepping into the shower behind Liz.

"Did you think it was okay to have coffee with Jacob?" I bite out.

My eyes roam Liz's perfect body, and I can't control my cock. I'm hard as a fucking rock. My thick shaft is already dripping precum. I give myself a firm tug while I try to decide if I want to punish her or just fuck her for my pleasure.

I followed Jacob Hallmark all day today, trying to figure out his routine and see if he is handicapped. I wouldn't put it past the fucker to fake being a cripple. He's just that much of a low-life to pull some trick like that.

All I need is a small amount of evidence that tells me he started the fire. The fire that almost killed my dad. Getting that evidence will be enough for me to take his life, and this time, I'll make sure the job gets done. Nothing will be left when I'm finished with him. He's going to suffer a slow and painful death by my hands.

When I realized he orchestrated running into Liz, I wanted

to yank him out of that fucking wheelchair and rip out his throat. Maybe the next time I see him, I'll do just that.

Regret settles in the pit of my stomach for bringing her, but I couldn't protect her if she hadn't come. I couldn't leave her unprotected, and I don't trust anyone not to fuck her. She's beautiful and innocent. Too innocent for the likes of me, but she's fucking mine, and it's going to stay that way. I won't have another man's filthy hands touching what belongs to me, and Liz is Mine.

Liz doesn't realize how beautiful she is, which makes her even more gorgeous. She doesn't realize that I've sat in many dark corner booths watching the men approach her in clubs, the way their greedy gaze tracked what was mine. The lust in their eyes made me feel positively homicidal.

When they didn't make it back to her with a drink or from the restroom, she didn't know I followed them and threatened them within an inch of their life if they returned. I'm not sharing her with anyone.

Something in me snapped when I saw her through the window sitting at a table with Jacob. I can't stand to see her with any other man, and I know Jacob's type. I know he's very much attracted to my Liz. Jacob and I were good friends growing up. We ran with the same crowd. It wasn't often, but we shared girls.

All that changed when he betrayed me. Betrayed my family's trust. I can still remember the day our friendship turned into acid, eating my insides out of hatred for him. I was suppose to meet him for a night out, but instead of finding a friend waiting for me at home, I found him trying to fuck my sister—though saying he was trying to fuck Caoimhe was being too fucking generous. He was trying to abuse my blood, take from her what she wasn't willing to give him. Caoimhe had made it home before anyone and opened the door to let in our family friend... my friend. Tears stained her face as she begged me not to hurt him, not to tell our parents about Jacob attempting to rape her.

When I cut ties with him, Dad questioned me. Why weren't we friends any longer? I couldn't tell him because I gave my word to my sister. I'd do anything for the women in my life, even lie down my own life.

I suck in a breath when Liz turns around. Her perfect pink nipples are pebbled, begging to be bitten and sucked.

"Why am I here? Why couldn't you just let me go?" she questions, and I notice the redness in her eyes.

I can't tell her the truth. I can't tell her I want no one else but her. That no one else brings my cock to life like she does. How crazy and unhinged I feel when I'm away from her for longer than a day. My heart wants to tell her everything, but I don't want to risk her life. If anyone, even Jacob, finds out, I know they would hurt her to hurt me.

"I told you." I grab her by the jaw and bring her forward. "Your mouth pleases me, this sinful, perfect wet mouth." I tilt her head up, so I can close the gap and press my lips to hers. She might be angry, she might be upset with me, but beneath it all? She's mine, and she knows that inevitable truth as much as I do. That much becomes more than evident as my perfect, submissive pet melts beneath the weight of my kiss, giving in and kissing me back as if she craves me, needs me as much as I need her.

Running my hand up into her blonde hair, I pull her head back. Breaking our kiss, so I can trail my lips along her jaw and down along her perfect skin, I bite her neck. She moans, and it makes my dick twitch. I work my way down to her pink pebbled nipple. Pulling at it with my teeth, I hear her gasp.

"Oh, Liz, tell me, does that feel good?"

Eyes half closed, she moans, "Yes."

I get down on my knees and pull one of her legs over my

shoulder. Bringing her pussy to my face, I inhale the scent of her arousal.

"You smell so good."

Running my nose along her pussy, I lick my way up to her clit and give it a gentle tug with my teeth. She gasps and pushes her cunt even closer to my mouth, practically begging for it.

"Fuck Liz, your pussy tastes like paradise, and I never want to leave."

I grab my cock, fisting it as I continue to pleasure her, sucking on her clit hard as she rocks her hips back and forth. She's trying to take her own pleasure from me like the needy thing she is, and I might just let her do it. Her chest heaves, and I reach up, squeezing her breast with one hand while I continue to lick and suck her clit.

Her moans get louder, and her hands run through my hair, tugging and pulling, dragging me closer to her dripping pussy. She doesn't need her words to beg for her pleasure when her body begs so beautifully already.

I know she's close, so I flick her clit with my tongue, once, twice, then Liz screams, and that's all it takes for her to fall apart, pulling my hair while I lap up every drop of her orgasm with my tongue.

"Oh, fuck!" Liz says while trying to catch her air.

Getting off my knees, I turn her around.

"Bend over and grab your ankles."

I can't wait any longer to have what's mine. As soon as she follows my order. I thrust my cock inside of her. Her pussy is still spasming around me with the orgasm that hasn't even finished. I need to feel her walls around my cock, making every thrust that much better as I remind her who she belongs to.

"Fuck yes!" I feel like an animal as I roar my satisfaction, each thrust setting the beast inside me that was awakened, seeing her with Jacob.

Liz's pussy fits my cock perfectly. I slap her on the arse as I plow into her from behind. My balls slap against her wet pussy with each hard thrust. It doesn't take long for the same mind-blowing feeling to occur, making my balls draw up, and I feel the familiar tingle starting at the base of my spine. With one more hard thrust, I push into Liz, holding her tightly by the hips as I come in her tight cunt. Pulling out, I spread her apart, watching my cum drip from her pussy, my ownership running down her thighs. Wrapping my arm around her waist, the other is on her waist.

"Stand up, *M'Aingeal*," I say with gentleness. When she stands, I bring her flush against my body, letting our bodies draw strength from one another. I softly kiss her temple as I reach over her to grab the shampoo and pour some into my hands.

When I'm satisfied with the quarter amount of shampoo, I run my hands through her long strands of hair, making sure to lather up while rubbing my fingertips along her scalp.

"I don't want you around Jacob Hallmark."

"I ran into him. He offered me coffee. I didn't plan on it," Liz says softly. "You're hurting me!" Liz winces. I hadn't even realized that just thinking about that leech anywhere near her had made me tighten my grip painfully on her hair.

I try to relax, massaging her scalp in silent apology for hurting her without intending to.

"I don't want you to speak to him again."

"Mark, I can't be rude. If he speaks—"

"This isn't up for discussion. Don't speak to him. Don't have fucking coffee or tea with him, period. He's not a good man."

Liz exhales. "I thought you said you would share me with him. Isn't that what you said?"

I turn her around and press her back into the cold shower wall.

"Your pussy is mine. You are mine. No one is going to touch you but me. No. Fucking. One."

****

Before the sun rises, I'm up, freshly showered, and watching Liz breathe softly with her blond locks spread over her pillow, looking like an angel. She's my angel, and I'm her devil.

I put the note I wrote on the night table, letting her know she's not to leave the manor without calling me first. Taking one last long look at my angel, I quietly slip out the door.

I've been home for two days and haven't gotten anything accomplished. I need to start my day early if I'm going to investigate what the fuck happened at the brewery.

CHAPTER FIFTEEN

Liz

I wake up with my body still buzzing from the brutal pounding I received last night. There's no denying that he can make my body hum with his rough hands as they roam over my breasts and find their way down to my pussy, making me weep for more.

A smile forms at the thought of last night, and I roll over to see a folded-up note on the nightstand. I can tell by the slanted handwriting who it's from.

He underlined my name twice, a telltale sign not to cross him. I hesitate to pick it up because of the scolding I received yesterday. I lie back on my stomach until, finally, my curiosity gets the better of me.

Grabbing the note, I open it, and my muscles tense up in annoyance. He's telling me not to leave the manor without letting him know. As if I'm a child and I must report to him. My anger peaks at the thought of having to answer him. I crumple the paper and toss it across the room. Rolling over, I lie on my back, thinking about my amber-eyed devil.

Do I really like his demanding ways and his need to never talk about what's happening between us? The only thing I know for certain is that I'm falling for him. His rough edges make me want to get in the car and drive far away from him, but my body craves his edge of darkness. It craves the way he steals his needs from me, punishing my body to find his pleasure. When my body explodes, he is quickly chasing after me. But do I want to be with someone who dictates my every move?

Putting my thoughts aside, I get ready for the day. I might stay around the manor, or I might not. Maybe subconsciously, I enjoy disobeying him.

Fifteen minutes later, I'm about to take the last step off the staircase when I hear a voice coming from the study. They're trying to whisper, but their voices bounce off the walls and sound louder than they intend, making me curious about what they're saying.

Slowly, taking one step after another, I ease over to the wall, leaning against it. I don't recognize the woman's voice, but I can tell by the tone of her voice she's nervous.

"I know, but I'm telling you, they don't know."

She pauses, and I can tell by hearing her footsteps she's walking in circles.

"I'll try!" she whisper-yells into the phone to whoever she's talking to.

When I hear footsteps approaching the door, I run on my tiptoes to the kitchen. Rounding the corner, I smell the most intoxicating aroma drifting into the hallway.

Popping into the enormous kitchen where the smell is stronger, I close my eyes and moan.

A laugh startles me.

"Oh, sorry." I look at what Aine, the cook, is preparing, "That smells delicious." I say as my mouth waters, "What is it?"

Aine smiles at me. "Potato pancakes. Take a seat. They're almost done.

"Yes, please."

Aine fills my plate and sets it in front of me. I dive into the large stack of pancakes.

The clicking of heels against the tile floor gets louder. Looking toward the door, I see the beautiful lady who was in New York with Mark at Rose's party, and my heart drops to my feet.

When she sees me sitting there, she smiles. "Hello."

My mouth is full of food, but I nod and swallow, taking a sip of my drink to wash it down. "Hello."

She walks over and takes a seat next to me. "I'm Caoimhe, Mark's sister."

His sister? The beautiful woman who was on his arm at Rose's party was his sister? Even after I told him to go fuck his date, he didn't mention that she was his sister. Why does he stay silent? Why doesn't he confide in me?

Why does she assume I know Mark? Did he tell her about me?

I peer up to see Roxy standing in the doorway, a smug grin on her face. Why is she here, and was that her that I overheard in the study?

Roxy struts in with the smugness still plastered on her round face. She's pretty and clearly a woman who knows what she wants. Her confidence oozes out of her with the way she holds herself.

Taking the seat next to Caoimhe, Roxy asks Aine for a plate.

Two more women walk in, and my jaw drops at their beauty. When they walk closer, I see the same amber color in their eyes Mark and Caoimhe have.

The women are chatting and laughing with each other, taking a seat across from Caoimhe and Roxy. I can tell by the way their eyebrows crease when their eyes rest on Roxy that they are not fond of her.

Good.

"Where are your manners?" Caoimhe asks the young women.

They introduce themselves as Mark's sisters, Ciara and Clodagh.

Something strange hits me in the heart, making me envy Mark. He has a large, normal family who loves him and an upbringing in a home that's larger than the crappy apartment complex I lived in with my crackhead mother.

Lost in my own thoughts, I feel a soft touch on my hand.

"Liz," Caoimhe says, and I can tell she's the mother hen of the sisters. "You seem miles away."

"Maybe she's out of her league here," Roxy sneers.

"Roxy!" Caoimhe barks.

When Caoimhe gives Roxy a hard glare, I can tell there's a harder side to Caoimhe. A side that is too much like her brother.

"We need to go," Caoimhe remarks, looking at the twin beauties sitting across from her. "I have more orders than I can do in a day."

"What do you do?" I can't help my curiosity, wanting confirmation if their family is normal or if they're into shady business.

"I have an online company. A boutique store, you could say." Caoimhe smiles.

I swallow.

I doubt selling clothes is the line of business she's in.

When all four women get up to leave, I'm reminded that I'm just a guest in their home.

I watch them like an outsider, and my skin crawls at the thought of how close Roxy is to Mark's sisters. It could be so easy for one of them to talk him into getting with her. Would I be relieved if he did?

CHAPTER SIXTEEN

Mark

The sound of crushed ashes is magnified with each step I take, piercing my heart. The wind blows, lifting the ashes up, swirling them around me, and steals them, carrying them off into the distance, reminding me that dreams can be destroyed.

It leaves me wondering if I hadn't left, would this have happened? Would I still be standing here today with these emotions of lost time? Time lost between a father and his son. Emotions that I don't like to feel are spinning around, causing me to doubt my life. Doubt what I do to live. Having Liz here is not helping.

No. I shake my head. Those doubts are not what is bothering me. It's the thought of my pride making me stay away for so long. The same pride that runs through my father's veins—his pride of not reaching out to me to want me to come home.

I look around, soaking in the explosion's aftermath. The fire burned down the back of the warehouse, leaving the office covered in a heavy dust of smothered dreams—years of hard labor gone.

Looking down at the report in my hand, I exhale. I've been

reviewing the report for an hour. I can't find one single bit of evidence that stands out. Nothing. My thoughts are scrambled, and I know why. It's Liz. Unexpected feelings are occurring within me. The want to have her in my bed day and night, to hear her moans and feel her wetness on my cock. The urge to have her lips glisten from my cum every day is becoming a desire that will cost her or me. I want to protect her at all costs from the enemies I've made.

There's a car honking outside. I grab a nearby napkin. It's not clean, but it'll do when I wipe the soot off the window. My soul goes cold, preparing itself to do whatever damage it needs to take care of. I grind my teeth.

Fucking Jacob. How the fuck did he find me?

I stuff the paperwork in my back pocket and leave the office, heading to the front door. I don't want to give Jacob the satisfaction of seeing more than he should with the destruction of O'Brian Brewery.

When I open the front door, I see Jacob's driver lowering him down in the wheelchair. My anger spikes when we make eye contact, and he places a smug grin on his ugly face. I grip the doorknob so hard, it breaks in my hand. It takes all I have not to beat the ever-living fuck out of him. I have to keep telling myself it wouldn't be a fair fight. But when have I ever cared about fairness?

"Brother," Jacob bellows.

My body tenses at that word—brother. We were like brothers at one time, a long time ago.

"Don't fucking call me that. We're nothing to each other," I command.

Jacob tilts his head, the corner of his mouth rising into a smirk.

The bastard.

"You'll never be anything to me other than the low-life you are. After you tried to rape my sister, we are nothing to each other."

He clicks his tongue and slowly shakes his head, disciplining me like I'm a fucking child.

I want to unleash my rage on him. I step forward only to have his oversized driver meet my step.

"Everything that comes out of Caoimhe's mouth is not gold, brother." He spits out the word 'brother' like it sits too heavy on his tongue. He smiles. "Now, what she can do with that mouth." His eyes change, something that I've never seen in him before. Admiration? "Is gold."

I launch forward. His driver blocks me, but I'm still fighting. Hatred fills my soul for this piece of shit.

"I know what I saw." I feel my jaw locking up from all the tension, making my ears ring and my vision darken with violence. "Leave. You're not fit to step onto my family's land." I pull back. I will get what I need and visit him when he sleeps.

"I just wanted to wish you and your family my condolences." He pauses, looking around at the old brick building that holds our office. Later, they added the warehouse, which now lies on the ground in a pile of rubble. "It's a shame. All those years of hard work."

He actually tries to look remorseful for our so-called unfortunate luck, but when that smug grin appears on his ugly face again, I know he's behind the fire.

My father is proficient. Staying on top of everything that has anything to do with the family business, not only with business but with family. Everything but his relationship with his only son.

Once Jacob leaves, there's a black cloud hovering over me, making me doubt my sister, Caoimhe. I think back to what Jacob said about my sister. Maybe I don't know Caoimhe. I see her when she visits, but maybe I need to be more careful. Betrayal is not a forgiven sin, not when it's family. I pull out my cell from my slacks and dial Sean.

Sean is my inside contact in Cork. He's been an associate I can trust, someone I know will have my back. Unlike Jacob, Sean would do nothing to cross me.

"Marcáil," Sean answers in a welcoming tone.

"Seán."

"It's been a long time, my friend. I heard you were back and accompanying a beautiful lady."

Fuck! How does he know about Liz?

"You're awfully quiet, my friend. I'm guessing I've heard right. You have a steady fuck." He laughs. "Never thought I would see the day Mark O'Brian would settle with only one woman."

He's right. I've never thought of myself as being with one woman, but Liz differs from anyone I've ever known. She's hard on the outside, but on the inside, she's broken. Something inside of me wants to fix her, but she's put up a damn brick wall I'm unable to break through.

"You bring her by the club. Drinks are on me," Sean insists.

Bringing Liz around any of the men I know is not wise. Sean will try to use his sweet words to get her naked on her knees, sucking his cock, and that shit just isn't going to happen. The only cock her tongue will wrap around is mine. I grit my teeth and try to cool my temper.

"Sean," I speak harshly. "I need you to put a tail on Caoimhe."

He laughs. The fucker laughs hard and loud.

"You finally caught on to your sister's ways, huh?" Sean asks.

I want to ask him what the fuck he's talking about, but I don't. The thought of my sister being into shit like me doesn't sit well. I want to shield my sisters from men the likes of me, from the life I live.

"Arrange it. I want to know where she's going and who she's with." I hang up while he's still fucking laughing.

I need to make one more stop before I head back to the
manor.

CHAPTER SEVENTEEN

Liz

Jealousy is an ugly feeling. It's a poison that runs through your body, rotting your insides. It's a feeling that I shouldn't have, especially when it involves a man like Mark.

After Mark's sisters and Roxy leave, I sit at the table, finishing my breakfast. I have no plans for today, and since Mark demanded I stay at the manor, I'm guessing I won't be able to leave without being told I can.

"What are your plans for the day, sweetie?" Aine asks.

I chew my food, trying to find the right words. Is she asking to report back, or is she being genuine?

"I'm going to hang out by the pool," *Unless* … "Or go into town. Do you know if I can call an Uber?" I don't want to sit in this place all day or hang out by a pool. Maybe I want to be punished, or it might be that I don't want to obey Daddy Mark. Either way, fuck it. I'm doing what I want to.

"Uber? We don't have those, but you can call a taxi. Are you wanting to go into town?"

"Yes, I was thinking about taking Caoimhe lunch. Can you give me her shop address?"

I wasn't planning on taking them lunch, but it's a great

excuse, and I would like to see what type of business she's in.

Aine writes the address and hands it to me. She also tells me about an app that I can use to arrange for a taxi. After I download the app, I schedule a pickup and drop off.

Running upstairs, I walk into our bedroom and grab a small shoulder bag, ensuring I have my ID in case someone decides to off me. My passport is gone. It doesn't take a rocket scientist to figure out who took it. I already know by the smell of his rich cologne lingering in my purse.

Of all the nerve.

Angrily, I storm out of the bedroom, glad that I'm disobeying him. I hope Aine calls him and lets him know I have left the manor, disobeying his endless commands.

Thirty minutes later, I'm sitting on the concrete steps in front of the manor. I look off in the distance and see a silver four-door car coming down the gravel drive between the neatly trimmed hedges.

A sign hangs on the door, reading Taxi. When it stops in front of me, I can see the driver. His expression is sour. He rolls the passenger window down.

"You sit in the back," he commands.

Rude.

Nevertheless, I hop in the back with a smile spreading across my face. When the car pulls away, I smile even brighter.

Fuck you, Mark!

When the car pulls up in front of a building, I know we're at the address I gave him. It's not quite run down, but it's not in a newer section of town, which surprises me.

Reaching up front to the driver, I hand him a tip. He takes it and sneers at me.

You're lucky you're getting that much, fucker.

When I'm out of the car, I reach for the door to close it. Thank goodness I pull my hand back in time because the driver takes off.

It's still early and not quite lunchtime, so I have time to kill before entering the shop. There's a cute little red café across the street, which almost looks like an oversized phone booth.

Looking both ways, I cross the street. Going inside, I sit at a table in front of a large picture window. A teenage girl walks over and takes my order. I only order water because I'm so full from Aine's delicious breakfast.

Turning my attention back to the view from the window, I stare at the shop across the street. There's no indication of a shop inside the small space, no signs, no welcome mat, nothing being displayed in the windows. I wonder why she doesn't advertise.

I bet my suspicions are true, and she's not into anything legal. Illegal behavior must run in their family.

Random thoughts of Mark enter my mind, wondering what he was like as a young boy and why he doesn't come home to live with his family.

It's not long before a sleek black car pulls up in front of the building, and Caoimhe emerges. The back door opens, and she disappears into it. I can't make out who's inside. The windows are tinted too dark.

I quickly pull out my cell. When the car pulls away from the curb, I wait until I can get a good view of the license to snap a picture.

My fingers linger over the keys. I could send it to Rose. She could get Blaze to get the information for me, but do I want to chance Mark finding out I'm snooping?

When I hit send, I know there's no turning back. Quickly after sending the picture, I text Rose.

I need a favor. Can you find out who's tag this belongs to?

Rose replies back. *Is everything okay?*

I try to think of something to say. Rose has always been good at reading me and determining if I'm lying to her.

Lunchtime comes around quickly. Calling the waitress back over, I order a few sandwiches and a couple of side items to go.

Once the employee comes out with a large sack and I pay for the meals, I give myself a mental pep talk and head across the street.

Opening the door to the small shop, what I see inside surprises me. There's nothing out of the ordinary. The space has a large open floor plan with four large white oak desks strategically facing one another. Clothes are lined up on a rack and neatly stacked on shelves.

"Liz, this is a nice surprise," Ciara or Clodagh says. I think it's Ciara. She has the warmest smile out of the twins.

I swallow the lump in my throat, hoping they buy my lies.

"I wanted to bring everyone lunch today," I announce with my best smile, which isn't hard to do. Ciara is a sweet girl. She has a welcoming personality.

Ciara and Clodagh are my age. They have long dark hair that frames their faces, with amber eyes that sparkle, just like their brother.

Mark's sisters are filled out with voluptuous curves that make them stand out in any crowd. All the sisters, except for Grace, which makes me wonder why she's not as filled out as the others. Maybe she takes after someone in the family with a small frame and petite size.

Clodagh stands. "Thank you, I'm starving. Caoimbe works our fingers to the bone while she's out doing..." She stops herself and clears her throat.

Ciara starts talking right where her sister left off. "What did you bring us?" she asks, making her way over to look in the bags.

I walk to her and hand the bag off. "Where is Caoimbe?" I look around and notice Roxy is nowhere in sight, but I know I didn't see her leave through the front door, "And Roxy?"

"Roxy delivers orders to several of the boutique stores we work with," Clodagh says casually. "She doesn't work for us full time, just some of the time."

I make small talk with the twins while they eat. After lunch, I'm about to pick up my bag and leave when a very disheveled Caoimhe walks in the front door. She looks all shades of being very well fucked. Her hair, which normally hangs down her back like silk, has strings of hair sticking out in all directions. Her makeup is worn off in spots, and her mascara is smeared across her eyes. I would say Caoimhe has definitely been very well fucked.

"Did you grab yourself a sausage dog?" Ciara asks Caoimhe with a smirk.

"Mind your business," Caoimhe huffs.

The twins look at each other and laugh.

It must be an inside joke because I don't understand what is funny.

Placing my bag over my shoulder, I tell the ladies, "I'm off to do nothing."

"Stay with us," Ciara says. "You can help us process orders." Ciara gives me a warm smile that lets me know she's sincere, and I gladly accept.

***

I get to work after Ciara shows me how to process their orders and gather the items to bag.

I haven't seen Roxey all day and feel relief from not having to deal with her nasty attitude and the looks she gives me.

The doorbell rings. I look up, locking eyes with a very angry, large man. Mark. The steam is practically billowing out of his nostrils, and his chest heaves with each large inhale of air he takes.

He stalks over and stands above me. I have to crane my neck to look up at his intimidating face. I swallow, wondering if I made the right choice to disobey him. His silent threats pass in the air while his amber eyes burn through me.

CHAPTER EIGHTEEN

Mark

When I pull out of the driveway of the warehouse, dust plumes rise behind me, leaving the view in my rearview mirror hazy, much like my mind.

I'm driving over to see John Hallmark—Jacob's dad. I haven't seen the old man since returning, and Jacob's visit has unsettled me. I need answers. I know the Hallmarks can pull off an electrical fire, but are their souls dark enough to carry it through?

Thinking back to all those years ago when I overheard John and Jacob talking about destroying my family's company, I remember them talking about taking the business away from us. Is this how they would accomplish that goal? Have they been planning this all along?

I pull up to the house and park. The grounds don't look as manicured as they used to when I visited Jacob growing up.

Getting out of the car, I make sure to look around for guard dogs. John has always had large dogs to scare off any unwanted guests. When I see no indication of dogs, I head toward the door. The large steel frame stands before me as I raise my hand to knock. It swings open, and a short lady with gray strays of hair sticking out everywhere stands by the door.

"Is John around?"

"He's in the study." Her lifeless eyes look at me with an empty soul behind them. "What is your name, sir? I will see if he's available."

"Mark O'Brian." I don't give her anymore. I don't have to. He knows who I am and exactly what I can do.

After a brief moment, she walks back and shows me the way to his study. There is really no need. I practically lived here growing up. If I wasn't over here, Jacob was at my house.

When we stand in front of the door, the old lady gives me a nod. I reach out, opening the door. When I take the first step inside, I feel an uneasy deadness in the air.

I look up to see John sitting in his tall leather back chair behind his large red oak desk. My eyes narrow, studying him and his every move.

"Come in, Mark, sit," John says slowly with a raspy voice.

Strange. He looks and sounds frail.

After all these years of trying to take what isn't his, it's played hell on his health.

I sit in the small brown leather chair in front of his desk, carefully not taking my eyes off him.

He coughs. "What can I do for you, son?"

"Son," I scoff and raise an eyebrow.

He looks bewildered by my reaction.

"You've always been like a son to me, Mark. You know this."

He coughs again, but this time, I can tell it's a cough that could be a health concern.

"What's the matter, John? Are you dying?" I taunt.

John's eyes shoot up at me.

I widen my eyes. *Fuck, he is.*

"Does Jacob know?" Curious if he has told his fucked-up

son.

"No, and I would appreciate it if you stayed quiet about it. I haven't told anyone," John says quietly.

"Not even your loving wife?" I bite my tongue. That bitch is anything but loving. She has to be the worst unfit mum in all of Ireland.

"Orla passed away a few years ago," John says.

Well fuck, I didn't know.

I still say he's better off with the bitch gone, but if I had known, I wouldn't have said that.

"I won't say anything if you give me the answer I want. If you lie to me, I'll make sure your last days are living in hell."

John doesn't flinch, which surprises me a little. I wasn't aware if he was current on my dark reputation.

Instead, he opens a drawer and sets a box of Cohiba Behike cigars on his desk.

"Take one," John says with much more energy in his voice.

"I'll pass." I'm not here to be his fucking buddy, and having a smoke together is not what I want to do with him. I would rather be breaking his bones and recording his screams so I can hear them in my sweet, dark dreams.

John pulls out a straight cutter and snips the end of the cigar. Sticking it in his mouth, he lights it up and inhales, then leans back into his chair and blows out the smoke.

"Let me guess. You think I have something to do with the fire in the warehouse." He looks way too smug.

"Did you?" I ask, with death outlining my words.

"I have no desire to take anything away from your family." He draws on the cigar. "I have no interest in hurting anything that would hurt Grace."

My jaw locks. He said Grace's name a little too sweetly.

"Why would you care about anything concerning my sister?"

"I'm an old man, Mark. I'm dying, and there's a time for

everything. I think you should speak to your mum instead of asking me."

"What does my mum have to do with you speaking so fondly of my baby sister?" My nostrils flare. "My sister's name shouldn't even come out of your dirty mouth, Old Man."

John doesn't seem fazed by the threat in my voice. He doesn't seem to be challenging me, either.

"Mark, I've survived a crash that should have taken my life but left my son paralyzed. Do you have any idea how that feels?" He tilts his head. "Do you?"

I don't say anything.

"All those years ago, and the crash still haunts my dreams. I have a feeling I know who cut those brake lines, and I don't think it was your dad. Only one person I know is as evil as Satan." He raises an eyebrow. "Don't worry. I have no intention of starting a war between you and Jacob. It would only hurt... others. Jacob needs...." He pauses for a brief moment, looking off at the wall. "Jacob will need what little family he has left."

What the fuck is he talking about?

"We're not family, Old Man. We'll never be family." I bark out.

"Grace—" He stops. "You need to talk to your mum. I'm done with this conversation. I need to rest." John carefully eases out of the chair, ignoring me, and walks out of his study.

I'm left with my thoughts of what the hell is going on and why he keeps saying Grace's name. I came here to help with my family's company, but now I've had so much more dumped in my lap.

Once I leave the Hallmark's, I'm on the road heading back to the manor.

I pull up, walk inside, and go straight to the kitchen. I know Aine will know exactly where Liz is. Walking into the kitchen, I don't see Aine, but I see my mum. She's sitting at the table in the breakfast nook, looking over some papers. I pull out the seat next to her. Getting a glance at the paperwork, I see they're insurance forms.

"I can take care of those for you."

She raises her head as if she's just noticed me. She starts to speak, then closes her mouth. Her eyes hold emotion, and I can see her tears building up.

"Tell me," I say softly, taking her hand. I don't like seeing my mum hurt. I know she's dealing with a lot with my dad being in a coma.

CHAPTER NINETEEN

Mark

There's a stiffness in the air. The void in my mum's silent words raises more questions.

Mum has always been a strong woman. Taking care of her family and doing it all with a skillful hand that only a few women possess.

"Tell me, Mum," I ask again with a little more sternness in my voice. I don't want to use a forceful hand, but this feeling of a hidden secret makes me angry. When her eyes don't hold mine, I inform her, "I went to visit John Hallmark today." Looking at her face, I wait for any sort of reaction. I see her tells before she even opens her mouth. She swallows, and her hand starts to shake.

"It made me uneasy how he mentioned Grace's name. Any ideas why he would speak her name?"

She doesn't look up to meet my eyes. Instead, she sets the papers she's holding on the table, then, places her palms flat against them. I can see she's clearly shaken and trying to steady herself. A tear rolls down her cheek and falls off her chin to land on the insurance forms.

I give her a minute to let her gather herself. Whatever is

bothering her has something to do with Grace, and I want to know what the fuck it is. I need to find out if all these lies and hidden secrets are why my father is lying in a coma.

Mum looks at me with her eyes glossed over but doesn't say anything. Instead, she turns her head slightly, looking beyond me. I feel the presence of someone standing nearby. I turn and look behind me to see Grace standing in the large door frame, confusion on her face.

"Grace..." I pause. I don't want her to know how much Mr. Hallmark cares about her well-being. It sickens me to think of that old man wanting my sister. "We were talking about Father."

She doesn't reply. She stands in the doorway with a blank expression on her face.

I wonder how much she heard.

"I was coming in to grab a bottle of water." She walks to the fridge to open it but pauses and turns back to us. "I went to see Liz, but I can't find her. I wanted to know if she wanted to go out to grab a bite for dinner. If that was okay."

Fuck!

Aine comes into the kitchen with a basket of vegetables. She must have been out in the garden when I first arrived.

"Aine, where is Liz?"

Aine sets the basket down on the counter. "She went to see your sisters." She pulls the vegetables out and starts to wash them.

When I don't speak, she looks up to see my reprimanding frown.

"Mark... Sir, I..." Her throat works up and down. "I thought it would be okay."

"It's fine, Aine," I ball my fist up. "Mum, we will talk about this when I get home." She nods. I will have to deal with my mum later. Right now, I need to get to Liz. Aine may not have known that I ordered Liz to stay at the house, but Liz knew, and that's where she made her first mistake.

***

I arrive at the little shop where my sisters work. Walking across the concrete crosswalk, the sound of my heavy footsteps bounces off the ground and vibrates my ears.

The doorbell rings when I open the front door, sending an alarm to everyone that someone has entered the shop. Liz's eyes cast up. I slam the door shut, and with determination in my gait, I stalk over to her.

She's working, and even though I know she's doing something for my sisters, I'm still pissed at her for not staying put. Our eyes never veer from one another, and I know she can see the enraged demon behind the blazing flames in my eyes.

Bending down, I try to give off the persona of a caring lover. I reach out to lock my large hand around her upper arm. It may look like a gentle touch, but it's anything but. Raising her up from her seat, I give her arm a squeeze, reminding her that she's fucked up and that I'll be her personal god, handing out her judgment. She doesn't cause a scene. I must give her credit for that.

Liz gives me a smile that could kill the actual devil himself.

"Oh, Mark," she says with distaste. She brings her mouth to my ear and whispers, "I missed you just as much as I miss the cockroach I killed this morning." She laughs and kisses me on the cheek, sending a silent message to my sisters that everything is okay.

Fuck, why does this woman drive me mad? The way she hates me but loves my cock drives me fucking insane.

"*M'Aingeal*, you have the cock part right," I say, not giving a damn who hears me. "We have missed you and that sweet mouth of yours." I grind my teeth when I say those words. I have missed her. Missed being inside of her, but right now, all I want is to take my belt to her arse.

Her face goes blood red, but she keeps her mouth shut. I

111

smile with ease, knowing I'm ruffling her feathers.

"No, Mark," Liz spits my name out in disgust. "My devil." She puts her lips to my ear, and when her sweet breath tickles my neck, my dick twitches in my pants. "You can suck your own dick tonight. I have plans with your sisters."

"Not tonight. I have plans for us." I escort her to the door and right to the passenger seat of my car. Buckling her up, I grab her chin and pull her lips to mine. I pull back, sucking on her bottom lip. "I'm going to enjoy tonight. I'm already hard for you, *M'Aingeal.*"

I shut the passenger door and go to the driver's side. When I get in, she doesn't say a word.

Good.

***

When we arrive at the manor, Liz jumps out of the car and tries to run from me. I laugh out loud and watch her scramble away. She's not going anywhere. Making it inside, I see her at the top of the grand staircase.

A noise captures my attention. When I see a light in the study, I pause—coming closer to the door, I can see through the crack of the opening. I can make out it's a female, and they're shuffling through drawers.

I grab the handle and swing the door open. My mum gasps when it hits the wall, and she puts her hand on her chest.

"Mark, you scared me."

"What are you looking for?" She looks guilty, and I can't help but wonder what she is trying to find so desperately. Does she have something to hide?

"Hmm …" I can tell by the way her face contorts she's trying to think of something to say. "I'm looking for the certificates that show proof of insurance on the brewery. I need to copy and send them in with the forms. You know, the forms that I was looking at earlier."

I sit down in front of my father's desk, "Do you need help?" I'm trying to corner her to see if she's lying.

"No, I don't see them. They must be in the safe."

Her words sing a song, and I need answers.

"Why does John Hallmark seem to be so concerned with Grace's well-being?"

She stops dead in her tracks, looking for whatever she's supposedly looking for. When she faces upward to look at me, I can see she's pale.

"I don't know what you are talking about."

She's lying, and I can see it.

Jumping out of my seat, I throw my fist down so hard, the desk cracks where it lands.

"Don't lie to me. You don't want to know what I do with liars." I give her a minute while she works her throat. She needs to make sure the truth is spoken with the next words that come out of her mouth.

She exhales and leans back into the leather seat as if she's been defeated.

"John Hallmark is Grace's biological father."

I breathe in a large amount of air and fall back into the seat.

"Fuck!"

We stare at each other.

"How did that happen?"

"Your father and I were having... problems. Mark, it was one time, and I have regretted it ever since, but I don't regret having Grace. She put us back together again. When I found out I was pregnant, we talked through our issues. Being married at such a young age..." She pauses. "We didn't get to see out the plans we each had for our life, and having children strains your marriage. I love your father. I wouldn't change anything, but John was there when I felt alone when your father worked day and night."

"Did his wife know?"

"No one knew. Please, Mark, don't tell Grace. Your father and she have always had a close relationship. It would kill both of them if they knew."

I scrunch my brows. "Why the hell would you keep a secret like that from your own husband?"

"I was just protecting Grace. I didn't want her to find out after all these years."

My head spins from all the deception.

When I start to rise, Mum begs me, "Please, Mark, not a word."

"I won't speak a word, but if you don't tell father when he comes out of that coma... I will." I walk out without saying another word.

Heading in the direction of my bedroom, I shake my head. When I walk into the room, I watch Liz run into the bathroom and hear the door click.

She's locking the door. Does she really think she can keep me from coming in?

I reach above the door and grab the key that rests on the door frame. When I open it, she's standing in the corner, looking every bit like a small child about to get in trouble.

At least she knows what her sin is.

My eyes are fixed on her as I stalk across the tile floor, and I can't help the feeling that passes over me. It's a warm desire to hold her, to kiss her, and to cherish her with such passion, she'll know I have fallen in love with her.

I close my eyes and breathe in. I need these feelings to disappear. Now is not the time. She needs to know I need her to do as I say for her own protection. I grab her by her throat and bring our lips close.

"I told you to stay at the manor today. Why did you disobey me?" I run the length of my nose against hers. "Answer me. Do you like being punished?" I feel her throat work. My grip is tight, but it's not hard enough to hurt.

"I didn't want to stay around the manor. I was bored."

In one swift motion, I turn her around to face the wall. My left arm holds her in place while I push her leggings down.

"Stop, stop," Liz begs.

Ignoring her plea, I continue to push down her leggings over her hips, letting them pool around her ankles. I draw my hand back and smack her on the arse as hard as possible. Liz yells out, thrashing against my hold on her.

Tears well in her eyes as she yells, "You monster. How can you be such a monster and come from such a loving family?"

I stop. The words she spit out slice through me, leaving me bleeding. It hurts. Never has anyone's words hurt.

CHAPTER TWENTY

Liz

After yelling at Mark, a cloud of remorse hangs over my head.

When I caught a glimpse of how his face fell, I could feel my heart falling with it. His soul may be tainted and his hands stained, but there's more to him that he doesn't share with anyone—a better side. A side that's buried deep down under the sheet of ice on his heart.

I should have known to keep his family out of my mouth and away from those ugly, lethal words. Throwing someone's family in their face is out of character for me. Even when I get angry, I don't use words that cut deep. Maybe it's due to my jealousy from having such a shitty mother and never knowing who my father was.

I meant what I said. How could someone have such a loving family and not be filled with the light that comes from their surroundings? I just should have kept those thoughts to myself.

His world in Ireland is filled with richness, love, and luxury. Mark could have so much more here, but he chooses a life of crime and a world without the love he could receive.

He turns me around and pulls our bodies flush with each

other.

When I turn my head to look up at him, I see a sadness in his eyes that wasn't there before, looking back at me. Part of me wants to ask him what's wrong. Is it the words I spoke, or is it something deeper?

I don't get the chance to speak because he softly presses his lips to mine. He kisses me, and this time, it's a kiss with tenderness. He reaches down my body and hoists me up. My legs automatically hook around his hips. He walks us into the bedroom while our tongues explore each other's mouths.

The kiss feels more... it feels... like love. Could that even be a feeling Mark could have?

Gently, he lays me on the bed with his strong, lean body hovering over me. His lips break away, and he kisses my chin, neck, and down my breasts.

His large, powerful hands, the same hands that commit sin after sin, are so soft and tender as he removes my blouse and roams them over my body.

"*M'Aingeal,* I want to protect you." He kisses me again, "Do you understand?"

Staring at him, I blink.

"Liz, Baby," he whispers. "Tell me you understand, and you will do what I ask."

Our eyes lock on each other. I take this sweet moment to soak in his soft ambers, shining like fresh, clean jewels. They're so vibrant, shining brighter than the darkness that lies behind them.

His eyes move back and forth over my face, looking, waiting, and searching for an answer.

I want to cherish this softer side of Mark. I want to see it so much more, and for the first time, I could see us having a life together.

I give him a slow nod.

He smiles, and I feel myself tearing down the block concrete walls around my soul and heart. This man drew me into his dark and depraved world. He consumes my mind, and he owns my body.

When he brushes his lips against mine again, it all feels different. There's passion and kindness that he's never shown. His tongue sweeps out and glides along my bottom lip, only to pull it away with his teeth.

I moan out loud. The painful ache between my legs is strong. Strong enough for me to raise my hips and grind myself against his erection.

"M'Aingeal."

Mark slides his hand down and rubs my pussy through my panties. I'm so wet for him. I want more, so much more. His touch feels so good.

My breath hitches. "Mark," I gasp.

His lips go to my neck, nipping and sucking my flesh. Goosebumps form on my arms, making me want his touch to be harder.

"Do you have wet dreams about my cock, about how it feels sliding in and out of this tight pussy?" Mark says in a deep voice that penetrates my core. "I dream about this beautiful pussy." He pulls my panties to the side and pushes a finger into me. "Wet, so fucking wet. Hmm. Fuck, my cock is so hard for you."

He pushes his hard erection into my leg, letting me feel his need and want for me.

"Mark... I need you inside me." I hastily tug at his pants, trying my best to unbutton them so I can pull him out, desperately wanting his cock.

"Whose cock pleases you?"

Mark makes circular motions around my clit with his thumb. A rush of desire hits me so hard, I grab his hand and push his fingers harder against me.

"You want it hard, baby?"

He pinches my clit, and I scream, "Yes!"

In a hasty move, he flips me onto my stomach and pulls my hips up.

Spreading me apart, Mark says in a voice laced with poison, "You want to take my cock in this,"—his fingers run along my pussy and back around to my back hole—"perfect arse." Mark slaps my ass. "Tell me." Another slap. "You want it dirty, don't you?"

My lips move, and the word comes out in a rush, "Yes, yes!"

I hear his zipper, then his cock is at the entrance of my tight back hole. I look around behind me to see his dark pupils. The yearning to fuck me consumes him.

"Don't worry, I won't hurt you… this time."

He pulls back slightly and spits down my crack. It trails down to my hole, and he spreads it all around with his fingers. He spits again, adding more lubrication, then slides one finger into my hole, in and out, in and out. It feels so damn good. He adds a second finger, speeding up the pace a little, scissoring them between thrusts as he stretches me for his cock. I am about ready to explode. He removes his fingers, and at that point, I know what he's about to do.

His cock, so thick with veins protruding through the velvet skin, pushes into the small tight ring of muscle, making me grit my teeth and pull on the bed sheets. His cock is so much bigger than his fingers.

The invasion of his hard cock causes tears to pool in the corners of my eyes.

Mark pulls my body up so my back is flush with his chest. Using one hand, he palms my breast, pinching and tweaking my nipple. He runs his other hand down my body, stopping at my pussy.

"I love how your body fits my cock perfectly," he whispers, placing a warm, soft kiss on my neck. "You and I were made for one another, *M'Aingeal.*"

I shiver. His words have me feeling all kinds of emotions—lust for him, sadness for the life I have endured, and the final nail in my coffin, love for a man I don't want to love.

In many ways, we are both our own kind of fucked up. My body doesn't allow my mind to think anymore when Mark's hand lands on my clit, and he starts to move his fingers in tight little circles.

His first few pumps in my body are slow. They hold affections of admiration, his lips soft and gentle on my neck. His desire and his need to fuck me like a two-bit whore takes over, and his pumps speed up, and his thrusts become brutal.

Mark removes his hand from my clit, smearing my juices over my stomach and up to my breast, giving it a hard squeeze, making me cry out loud.

"My beautiful dark angel. Tell me, do you like my cock?" He pivots his hips to flex his ever-hardened cock into my ass, and he hits the backside of my g-spot, making me cry out louder, but this time it's from pleasure.

He pumps one last time, making me fall off that cliff into oblivion. His hand holds my hips, emptying his seed into my back hole. When he jerks forward in an effort to push his cock into me even deeper, my body collapses to the bed, and I drop my head onto the pillow, trying to catch my breath. His assaults on my body take their toll on me, and I'm completely worn out.

Trying to catch my breath, I start to drift off when I feel the burn of Mark pulling out and hear the wrestling of him getting off the bed.

He spreads my ass cheeks and watches as his cum runs out and down the back of my thighs.

CHAPTER TWENTY-ONE

Mark

While I watch my cum run down Liz's thighs, something swirls around in my chest, squeezing my heart, leaving me trying to catch my breath.

It's a want and a need to care for her heavily within me. A feeling to take care of her.

I get off the bed and turn my head to look at her, noticing she's half asleep. Making my way to the bathroom, I turn on the hot water to get it warm, then reach for a hand towel on the shelf. I look at my reflection in the mirror, and I see it. I see the change taking place.

For the first time, I see a man in his later thirties wanting more. A family to call my own. A little girl with blonde hair and the cutest little nose, just like her mum. Maybe several little girls who would look just like Liz. I imagine Liz as a mum and know she would be great.

Ringing out the excess water, I enter the bedroom to find Liz completely asleep with her arse stuck up in the air. Just how I left her.

Her mouth is slack, and a hint of drool comes out of the corner of her lips. I chuckle. She must have been really tired between working today and afterward getting good and fucked.

I walk behind her and get the best view of her perfect pussy.

Pride surges through me, warming my insides. I'm the only one who's ever had the pleasure of having a taste and having my cock buried so far into her, feeling all her muscles as they milk my cock.

I start to clean her up when my dick starts to throb again. I can't help myself when I lean down and swipe my tongue, licking at her delicate flesh.

Liz moans, and I look up to see if she's awake. To my surprise, she's still asleep. I inhale her scent of sweetness and sex.

After discarding the hand cloth, I climb into the bed and bring Liz to me. She fits perfectly under my arm, with her head resting on my chest.

She belongs to me. *M'Aingeal*.

I wake up to the sun shining in my face and Liz's naked body flung over me. My dick is already hard, and wanting to slide into her heat, but I push back the urge and carefully pull Liz to the mattress.

I need to get a shower, but when I glance at my phone, I see I have a missed call from Blaze.

I return his call.

"Fucking hell!" he answers in a groggy voice. "You could have waited 'til a decent time to call. It's two in the morning."

I grin. I can imagine he's not been in bed too long.

"Too bad, fuckhead. I'm returning your call." I laugh a little when I hear him growl. "What's up?"

I hear noises and muffled voices in the background. I guess Rose is up now. I can't make out what they are saying, but they seem to be arguing. I hear Rose say no, don't, then Blaze comes back to the phone.

"Fuck," he pauses. "Shit, I didn't realize Liz was asking for…" Blaze stops speaking.

My heart rate picks up, and I'm not sure why, but I feel unhinged at the thought that passes in my mind.

Could she have had a run-in with someone in Ireland? Could her stalker from Maine have followed us?

"What was Liz asking?" I demand. My voice is shaky with thoughts of Liz in danger.

"She gave Rose a tag number and wanted to know who it belonged to."

I look over at Liz. She's still in a heavy sleep. Easing off the bed, I walk into the bathroom, shutting the door behind me.

"Give me the information." I can tell he's reluctant. Blaze is loyal to his wife, but our brotherhood will always remain close. I'm not concerned when he hesitates. I know Rose is lying next to him with a cold look. No doubt he will be in hot water when we get off the phone.

"Fuck," he comments. "Liz asked me to trace a plate number and wanted to know who it belonged to."

"And?" I wait further to hear what he's going to say.

"It belongs to a Jacob Hallmark."

My vision goes dark while I try to gain my composure. I squeeze the phone in my hand.

"Mark."

I hear Blaze, but I can't seem to snap out of the black cloud I'm lost in.

"Mark," Blaze yells into the phone.

"Yeah… I'll pass it on," I tell Blaze. Clicking the end button, I throw the phone into the wall, screaming, "Fuuuck!"

I punch the wall, putting a hole in the perfect décor of the bathroom.

The hole will go perfectly with the hole in my heart. Why would Liz be asking about Jacob? Why?

The door flies open with a disheveled Liz standing in the

doorway—naked.

"Mark," her eyes shift to the gaping hole in the wall. "What's wrong? Why did you punch a hole in the wall?"

My chest heaves. "Why were you asking for Jacob's tag number?"

Confusion is in her facial expression, but she's not fooling me with that innocent look. I know she's up to something.

I stalk toward her. Each step forward I take, she takes two steps back, hitting the doorway when she backs out of the bathroom.

"Wait, wait, Mark."

Taking one big step to her, I grab her upper arms.

"Are you looking for another cock to sit on?" Her eyes widen. "Or is it that you want to try to take me down with old Jacob," I taunt her. Pushing her back, I throw her down onto the bed. "Let me show you what happens to traitors."

Liz doesn't speak. She looks up at me with tears filling her eyes. Those tears won't get her out of this one.

I grab my belt off the velvet chair that sits close to the bed, folding it in half.

"Mark, please—" I cut her off.

"Roll over, Liz." My voice is thick with promises of pain. She doesn't do as I ask. Instead, she's trying to push her way backward, away from me.

I grab her small ankle, my hand wrapping around it so easily.

"Do what I fucking told you to do." Losing my patience, I flip her over while she starts to kick and curse at me. Drawing my arm back, I give her a small lick across the ass with the belt. She screams.

"That wasn't hard," I mock her. "This one will be harder." I strike her against the back of the thighs—hard.

Liz puts her hands over her upper thighs, trying to rub them.

"Move your hands." My voice booms with anger. Anger that she would have an interest in Jacob.

Her screams fill the air when I strike her thighs again.

"Tell me, *M'Aingeal,* why are you interested in Jacob?" She doesn't reply. "Another one?" I ask.

She shakes her head. "No," she yells as hiccups escape her throat. "No, I just wanted..."

The noise from someone trying to open the door knob grabs both of our attention.

"Liz, Liz, are you okay?" My sister, Grace, frantically asks from the hallway.

Liz's eyes search mine, and I raise an eyebrow, waiting for her to call for help.

CHAPTER TWENTY-TWO

Liz

I lie in pain as Grace rattles the doorknob, trying her best to open it.

It's no use. No one can save me from Mark. His anger radiates from him in waves, destroying everything in his path of rage.

Blaze must have called him. I should be irate over him ratting me out. Instead, pain surges through my body from the welts across my thighs and ass. A reminder that Mark will never be my hero. Instead, he'll be my nightmare. Staying with him will always have me walking on eggshells, trying to tiptoe around him to ensure that I never do wrong in his eyes.

Grace yells again, asking if I'm okay.

The thought of telling her no and causing her pain from seeing her brother at his worst is tempting, but I know in the end, it will only be my demise.

"I'm fine, Grace... just stubbed my toe... it hurt like a bitch. Sorry for yelling so loud," I lie as tears escape, cascading down my cheeks.

Mark doesn't show any remorse for the torment he's inflicted on me. Why should he? I have to keep reminding myself he's not the hero. He's the villain, and I'm his captive. Held against any hope of finding a life outside of his dark world. Outside of my own dark life.

He nods in approval of my response. I want nothing more than to strap the belt around his neck and hang him by it. I was a fool for thinking we could have something more than the lust between us.

Grace is quiet for a short period of time before finally speaking.

"Open the door, Mark. I want to see for myself."

My eyes go wide. Turning my head toward the door, I then look back at Mark, waiting to see what he'll say. Will he deny his baby sister, or will he show her who he really is?

"We're busy. Come back later."

"Open up, Mark!" She bangs on the door. "Now!"

He walks to the door, only opening it enough for them to get a small glance at one another.

"Grace, Liz is fine."

"Do you promise everything is okay?"

I love that about Grace. She's so sweet and innocent—a genuine kind heart.

"No harm will come to her. She will always be protected, don't worry. I take care of what is mine."

Mine. The words make me feel like an object.

She must have bought his act because Mark closes the door. He must be coming back to punish me more.

He leans down to me. "I want to know why you're asking for Jacob's tag number. Tell me, or you'll find yourself not being able to rest on your backside for a very... very long time." His voice is stained with promises of repercussions.

My throat is dry, and my voice is barely audible from the pain he inflicted on my body.

I swipe my tongue along my dry lips, "I saw Caoimhe get in a car and wanted to know whose car it was." I say in a rush. I hold back my words of how I don't believe his eldest sister is involved in more than a casual friendship with Jacob.

Mark's face falls, and by his expression, I can see that he knows. He knows his sister has her own secrets, but before he's able to confirm my suspicion, his phone rings.

"*Tá,*" he paces the floor, listening to the caller. "Where?" Not a minute later he slides the phone into his pocket.

"Stay here." He points his finger at me. Pulling a key from his pocket, he dangles it in front of me. "This time, you won't be leaving this room." A smugness stretches across his face. He turns, walking to the bedroom door. Before he has a chance to leave, I yell out.

"Wait!"

He stops to listen but doesn't turn to look at me.

"What if Grace comes back? You wouldn't want her to find me locked up, would you?"

Without a word, he opens the door and shuts it. I hear the turning of the key from the other side, locking me in the room.

My face falls onto the bed, letting my tears stain the sheets while I'm lost completely in my own insecurities. Why did I let myself fall in love with a man who only hurts me time after time? Allowing him to come back into my life only for him to inflict more pain on my body and mind. Will I ever mean more to him than just property? I thought last night we were finally getting somewhere, only to be fooled yet again.

He was so gentle and kind when we started making love last night. I still feel the touch of his lips placing soft kisses on my skin… until he turned back into the evil man I had come to know over the past years.

Maybe I'm more like my mother than I thought, falling for men who are no good for me.

With the soft sound of the door knob turning, I lift up to see if Mark has returned. Instead, Grace's angelic face peeks through. She gently closes the door, walking over to me with a disappointed look on her face.

"Liz."

She says my name so softly. I know she can feel my pain. The pain of loving her brother. Both physical and emotional. When she sits on the bed, she wraps me in her arms.

"I'm so sorry," she whispers. "I don't understand what caused him to do something like this to you. I know he loves you. I can see it in his eyes, his body language."

"Love? How can someone love and be evil at the same time? How can he come from a lovely family and be so cruel?"

Grace stares at me, processing what I've just said. After a brief moment, she finally speaks, shaking me to my core.

"His ways didn't fall far from his roots. You honestly don't think he's the only one in this family who has their hands stained in blood? There are secrets in this family only the walls know about, and they're not talking."

CHAPTER TWENTY-THREE

Mark

The ringing in my ears grows louder as I drive away from Liz. The feeling is a warning, telling me to prepare for the battles that lie ahead of me. The battles that I caused when I slapped my belt across her delicate flesh. Will she hate me? Does it matter to me if she does? She's mine, and I'll do whatever I need to do to make sure she stays that way—even kill.

I could've been easier on Liz, but the demon that lays dormant within me awoke with ferocity and was filled with jealousy.

Why would she be asking about Jacob's tag number? Does she not see how dangerous he is? Is she that naïve to go around snooping, trying to get herself hurt? I want to protect her, but how can I when she won't talk to me? She should be coming to me, not calling Rose.

My grip tightens around the steering wheel, knuckles turning white as my rage continues to build, thinking about how I should be the first person Liz wants to run to when she's in trouble. I wanted to tell her, show her how much she means to me. Instead, I allowed the demon in me to take over and inflict pain on *M'Aingeal*.

I slam my fist on the dashboard. A crackling noise sounds out, mirroring the crack in my icy heart. I never express my true inner self to anyone. I've always thought it was a show of weakness, and I wasn't going to allow anyone to hurt me. No one would ever hurt me, not like my father did so long ago.

This woman has made the beast inside my soul want to be a better man. I want to give all of myself to Liz. I know I need to hurry back to her. She must be confused about what my intentions are with her. To be honest, I've been confused too. All I know is that she's mine. She has always been mine. There is a possibility that she will close herself off to me for good. This time, I might have taken things too far with her. I have no one to blame but myself. But if there is one thing that I know for certain, it's that I will never let her go.

My mind has been occupied with thoughts of my beautiful *M'Aingeal* that time crept up on me, stealing the seconds with my drive to the hotel where Caoimhe is.

Sean called me, informing me that Caoimhe was meeting up with a man I despise. When he told me who she was meeting, my spine stiffened, and tension radiated through my body in violent waves.

She wouldn't meet him out of her own free will… or would she? Would she betray our family for a sleaze? He has to have something that he is holding over her head, forcing her to meet him at a hotel. I plan on finding out just what the hell it is.

When I pull the Audi up in front of the hotel, I immediately cringe. It's a shitty place, a place I can't imagine my sister would ever step foot into.

I spot Caoimhe's car alongside the old hotel. Her red convertible looks completely out of place with the rust traps parked beside it.

When I walk into the small lobby, there's an older man behind the front desk watching television. His skin has a yellow tint to it, leaving me wondering if he's been a lifetime smoker. The dark bags under his eyes let me know he must not sleep very much, if at all.

I walk up to the counter, but the man doesn't acknowledge my presence. I clear my throat to grab the old man's attention, but he doesn't even bother to look over at me.

What the fuck!

"He can't hear you," a lady with a grassy voice announces as she makes her way out of the door labeled storage.

"Is that so?"

"Yeah, he's deaf in one ear and can't hear shit out of the other." She coughs, and I can hear the cloud of smoke and tar coating her lungs.

"What can I do you for?"

"Have you seen her?" I pull my phone out and show her a picture of my sister. "I need to know what room she's in?"

The lady focuses in on the photo, squinting her cloudy cataract eyes.

I shake my head.

The woman stares at the picture. I know she can't see the photo. Her damn cataracts are so thick.

I'm growing impatient with the old couple.

"Can you see through those cataracts?" I ask harshly.

She shoots me a look. "Boy, I can see just fine."

A loud scream echoes through the floor above us, making everyone, even the deaf man, look up. When a loud crash occurs, I ask the old lady in a rush, "Where are the stairs?"

She points to a door, and I make a beeline to it.

I take the stairs two at a time. When I reach the second floor, I reach behind me, pulling out my Glock. I check to make sure the safety isn't on.

Pulling the door open, it slams into the sheetrock. Taking long strides down the hall in the direction of the screams, it's not long before I reach the door.

"You were supposed to be my friend!" Another loud crash occurs. "You stupid slut!" Another crash occurs.

I'd recognize that voice anywhere. Caoimhe.

I slam into the door, breaking it off the hinges. When it falls to the floor, it startles everyone.

Jacob is lying in the bed—naked. *Thank fuck he's got a sheet covering his dick.*

Caoimhe is standing on one side of the bed while Roxy is cowering on the other side, trying to cover herself with a shirt.

I look between the two women. Jacob is lying on the bed, clearly getting a kick out of having two women fighting over sucking his dick.

Fuck! My stomach churns at the thought of my own fucking sister sucking Jacob's dick.

"What the fuck is going on here?" I yell. I know what it looks like, but I don't want to acknowledge that my sister has been sleeping with this piece of shit.

Caoimhe's face falls, and she remains quiet. I can see she's not sure if she wants to answer me. She knows how I feel about Jacob. She knows I would consider it a betrayal to find out she's fucking him after what he pulled all those years ago.

I walk over to her and put my index finger under her chin, raising her head so our eyes can meet.

"Tell me, sis. Tell me you're not sleeping with him."

A tear runs down her cheek, giving her answer without words.

I want to spit out every word in the dictionary at her for being so naïve, but instead, I run my index finger up, swiping the tear. Looking down at the regret that leaves a stain on my finger, I bark off orders.

"Leave the room. Jacob and I have... things to discuss. I'll meet you at the manor in an hour. When I get there, you need to be in the study waiting for me." I'll deal with her in private.

I won't allow Jacob the satisfaction of fighting in front of him.

Caoimhe looks up with pleading eyes. "Don't, Mark. He didn't force me to do anything."

"What about when he tried to rape you all those years ago?" I look into her glassed-over eyes, emotions flickering behind her ambers. "He didn't try to rape you, did he?" I ask with a low growl.

When Caoimhe cast her eyes down, it all starts to fall together. Did it ever really happen? Or did I jump to conclusions and make up what I thought I had seen? Never would I want my sisters to choose to be with a man who has as many of the characteristics as me.

Caoimhe's face has sadness hanging over her like a dark cloud. She knows I broke my friendship with Jacob over her. I wanted to protect my sister, and I couldn't be friends with anyone who betrayed my trust. We were like brothers until that day.

Caoimhe and I never spoke of the day when I came home to find Jacob on top of her. It was unspoken words between me and Caoimhe. Now, I regret those unspoken words. I should have talked to her to find out what was really going on, but my pride got in the way, just like it gets in the way of showing my emotions to Liz.

"I just..." Caoimhe twists her fingers while trying to find her words. "I knew if I wanted to be with Jacob... you wouldn't approve." More tears escape, running down her pink cheeks. "I'm sorry," she whispers.

"Caoimhe,"—I inhale a large breath of air, steadying my heart rate—"I will deal with you when I get home. You need to leave. Go straight to the manor."

I silently wait to make sure Caoimhe has left the room. I can hear the soft sobs gently retreating down the hallway, which further pisses me the fuck off. Knowing she's gone, I turn my attention back to Roxy and Jacob.

"Roxy, it seems like you still like riding Jacob's dick, even after all these years. Do you think he will take you home to his daddy?"

Roxy glares at me. She's a good-looking woman, but her features are harder than they once were. They tell her story of living a party lifestyle. When she slits her eyes, I can tell I've hit a nerve. So, I keep going.

"Did you think his daddy would ever approve of this courtship? Tsk tsk. You poor deluded girl." I slowly stalk over to Roxy. She covers her body with a shirt, cornering herself against the wall.

Jacob watches us closely.

I wonder if I was to harm her, would he try to intervene?

When I get to Roxy, I place my hand around her scrawny neck. Jacob takes in a sharp intake of air—the pathetic sack of shit. How can he care for her over my sister?

"You didn't answer me. Do you still think Jacob's dad doesn't know what a low-life piece of trash you are? What your true intentions are?"

Her lips press in a thin line. She's furious with the way I'm talking to her. Good. Roxy thinks more of herself than anyone else does.

Roxy comes from the other side of our town. Her dad was a common thief, and her Mum didn't have a good enough education to get a proper job. She had to scrape to get by. Her family never had anything. They were poorer than most, but what set them apart was how they tried to con anyone and everyone not to have to work a real job.

Roxy tried to blend in with the kids who had money but never could. Everyone knew Roxy always wanted to be anything but who she actually was. That's the reason she hopped around on so many laps, riding any dick she could get to try to get married to someone who had money.

She reaches up, trying to pry my hand off her neck.

"Do you think your whore belongs better than I do?" she spits out.

My face drops. I can't hold back my rage any longer. I squeeze Roxy's neck hard, waiting for her soul to be taken to the only place that fits her best—hell.

"Mark, stop it!" Jacob yells to me, but I don't listen.

I want Roxy dead. At one time, I felt sorry enough for her to befriend her. No one speaks ill about my M'Aingeal.

I stare at Roxy as she slowly starts to lose the fight to save her pitiful life. When her face pales, I still hold on. Her hands drop to her sides, but I don't care. I can't seem to want to let go. I want to make sure her life has ended.

Arms wrap around me, trying to pull me away. My eyes blink, waking me up from the carnal rage surging through my body. I'm left speechless when I recognize whose arms are trying to pull me off. I let go of Roxy as her limp body falls to the floor.

Jacob pushes me to the side, fleeing to help Roxy.

What the hell! The mother fucker was supposed to be crippled. I'm left staring at a man who has led everyone to think he's been handicapped for years.

CHAPTER TWENTY-FOUR

Liz

Grace's words steal my breath.

More than one person has blood on their hands.

The words play on repeat in my head. Then the most disturbing thought passes over me. Could Grace have blood-stained hands, too?

Caoimhe, there's something dark and unsettling hidden in her eyes. The way she speaks is dominant. She's so much like her brother, the way she plays the role of a leader. I can also see a gentle part of her personality. When she thinks no one is looking, there's a sadness in her eyes, as though she's looking for praise from someone.

I'm so lost in my thoughts, Grace's laugh startles me.

"Don't be so naïve. I'm only kidding... maybe?" She says *'maybe'* a little too low and deep. It causes chills to run up my spine and steal the air from my lungs.

The room feels stuffy. Too stuffy.

I need time to myself—time to think about what to do next.

"I'm going to grab a shower. Do you want to wait here until I get out?" I try to be polite, but I really want to be alone.

"No, I just wanted to check in on you. I was just...

worried." She fumbles with the sleeve of her shirt.

I can tell she's wanting to say something. Placing my hand on hers, I say in an even tone, "Mark wouldn't hurt me."

Oh God, do I actually believe my own words?

Fuck, I must be as sick as he is. Maybe he's right. We do belong together.

Grace stands, pulling her hand away.

"His eyes hold a softness when he looks at you. He doesn't think anyone sees it, but I do. I see the affection in his eyes, but I know without a doubt if he thinks you'd ever betray him, he will hurt you. Just be careful with him." Her face is stern when she leaves me.

I stare at her retreating back, unsure how to decipher her intentions of warning me. My hands are clammy, so I wipe them on the sheet wrapped around me. The warning not to betray him still plays in my mind.

I hear the door click when I peel myself out of the bed and head to grab a shower. Entering the bathroom, I open the glass enclosure to turn the water on, letting it warm. I wait until steam fills the room before I drop the sheet and step into the large marble shower. The hot water envelops my skin, and I welcome the warmth until I spin around, and the stream of water hits the welts across my ass and thighs. The burn shoots straight through me, making me gasp for air. It's another reminder of Grace's words—not to betray Mark.

When I finish showering, I look for something to help ease the pain. Opening the cabinet, I see some salve that should help. I carefully apply it to areas I can reach.

While applying the cool lotion, I can't help but think about leaving. I need to run and leave Mark and his family. Maybe they're as crazy as he is. It seems they hold secrets from each other, and I don't want to be caught up in another family's drama when I've finally escaped the drama that has always filled my own life.

Graduating college and moving was my second chance in life. At least, I thought it would be.

If I run, will he follow me again? I let out a deep breath of air. Yes, he would follow me. I knew it before, and I know it more so now that he found me and wouldn't leave without me.

Walking into the bedroom, drying my hair with a towel, I notice Mark's suitcase in the corner near a chair.

I wonder if he has my stuff in it.

Pacing over to his suitcase, I lay it down and unzip it. Trying my best to search but not to mess up his belongings, I scan for my passport.

Reaching into the inside pocket, I feel it. When I pull the small hardcover passport out, my stomach flips with excitement. For once, lady luck is on my side.

Walking over to the dresser, I pick up my phone and hit the app for a driver. After placing a request for a driver, I quickly get dressed, grab my belongings, and leave down the hall.

Am I going to be able to escape without being noticed? I have to try. This house is as toxic as when I lived with Carla.

I freeze in my tracks when Carla's name pops in my head. I haven't thought about her since I left New York. Not once have I given her any thought. Guilt gnaws at me.

When I hear light footsteps coming up the stairs, it snaps me out of my guilt. I quickly make it out before being seen by ducking into the hall powder room.

Their footsteps are light, and I sense it must be a woman, but it's almost like they are trying not to be heard. My heart races at the thought someone could be in the manor without permission. Who could it be? Why would someone try to make their way without an invitation?

Stop overthinking, Liz!

Curiosity gets the better of me. Doing my best with a tight grip on the doorknob, I slowly turn it. I don't want to be heard and get caught. Explaining why I'm in the hall powder room with my suitcase would require a damn good lie.

I open the door ever so slightly, only far enough for me to see through the small crack. The tiny opening doesn't offer a large view, but I make out a shadow figure. Being brave, I ease the door open a hair more to see if I can catch a glimpse of their face, but I'm too late. They disappear in moments, and I'm not able to see who it is.

When a door slams, I jump, panic running through me. Closing the door in time when heavy footsteps crash outside, my blood drains from my head, making me feel lightheaded. I brace myself against the door, holding my breathe I slide down and try not to scream when I land on the hard marble floor that makes the welts left by Mark throb. The pain that burns on my behind brings tears to my eyes.

With tears in my eyes, I put my head in my hands, praying that whoever is in the house leaves and doesn't knock on the door. I shake my head, wishing I was anywhere but here.

CHAPTER TWENTY-FIVE

Mark

"Roxy," Jacob lightly taps her face. "Roxy."

He's squatting next to Roxy, pulling her head into his lap.

My anger builds as I glare at him. He's with my sister and Roxy, but the worst part is he's faking being crippled. I knew he was conniving, but to fake being crippled is a field on its own. His manipulative ways are ending today.

I grab his hair and yank him back from Roxy, who is rubbing her neck.

"You fucking piece of shit!" I growl at Jacob.

"Mark." His hands fly up, trying to hold on to my forearms.

"Don't. Don't you fucking dare beg for your life." I grab my knife from my back pocket and flick the blade open.

"Mark," Roxy pleads between grasps of breath. "It's not his fault. Please stop. Please."

I wrap my arm around Jacob's neck, hoisting him up to his feet. "Does my sister know you're not a cripple, mother fucker?"

He tries to answer, but I've got too much of a stronghold around his neck. I loosen my grip, allowing him to breathe. I want answers. I'm not ready to kill him yet.

"No…" he chokes out. "She doesn't." He coughs, trying to clear his air passage. "I wanted to tell her, but I couldn't yet."

"You couldn't or didn't want to?" I ask darkly.

He hesitates. I can tell his gaze is on Roxy. Tightening my hold, I squeeze his neck, letting him know I'm losing my composure and want my answer.

"O… kay," he wheezes out.

I let up on my hold to hear his next words. His hands are tight around my arm, trying to pull for relief.

"I couldn't. I was trying to wait 'til the old man died."

My brows pinch together. "Why would you have to wait?"

I know Jacob and his father haven't had the best of relationships, but I never thought he would go to the extreme of faking being in a wheelchair. And what would his motive be, faking such a thing?

"Let go of me, and I'll tell you," Jacob's voice barely audible.

Sighing reluctantly, I shove him onto the bed. "Sit up."

Roxy is still on the floor, but now she's in a sitting position, glaring at me. Her eyes dart to a nearby stool where her purse is perched on top, but I snatch it as she lunges forward.

I give her a smirk. "Stupid move."

When I fumble through the contents in the bottom of her handbag, I feel the cold, hard press of something metal. Pulling it out, it's a small handgun that fits in the palm of my hand. Sliding it into my pocket, I toss her the bag.

"Don't fucking move, or I'll shoot you with your own gun. Got it?"

Her lips draw into a flat line, not bothering to answer me.

"I'll say it again, and if you don't answer me, I'll go ahead and put you out of your miserable, pathetic existence. Nod if you understand what I'm saying."

There's an intense feeling in the air, and I can tell Roxy is pushing my limits.

Her eyes blaze with hatred for me, but I don't give a fuck.

She's still sitting on the floor, not bothering to answer my command. I draw her gun from my pocket. It's so small my hand engulfs it. I put the small barrel of the gun under her chin and tilt it upward.

From the swell of her breasts, rising and falling, and the panic flashing in her eyes, she understands her life rests in my hands.

"Yes, yes, I understand," she says in a rush.

"You should know not to fuck with me."

Jacob stares at Roxy, and there's a flash of something in his eyes I can't read.

"Jacob, stop looking at your whore and look at me." When his eyes meet mine, I don't recognize any concern or anger for me calling Roxy a whore. There's no emotion. His eyes seem like an endless void.

"Why my sister?" I spit out at him.

I want to know why, of all the women he's fucked, why would he want to be with my sister. We were close at one time. I made it clear to all my colleagues that my sisters were off-limits.

"Fuck, man," he shakes his head, then runs his hand through his shoulder-length hair. "She chased me. Before I knew it, she was riding my dick—"

"STOP."

My chest heaves with rapid breaths. No fucking body wants to hear about their sister riding any man's dick, especially not me.

"My sister deserves more than your arse cheating on her, especially someone with the likes of her," I point to Roxy.

"I'm someone, Mark," she spits my name out like it tastes bad on her tongue. "I'm his fucking girlfriend," Roxy barks out.

"No, you're not my girlfriend. How many fucking times do I have to tell you?"

"I'm out of here." Roxy stands, trying to gather her stuff.

I've had it with this bullshit. I pull out the sleek piece in my pocket, aim it, and fire it in Roxy's direction. The bullet slides past her earlobe, slicing through the outer shell of her ear. She screams like I sent it plunging into her heart.

Rolling my eyes at her over-dramatic reaction, I reach around the nape of her neck and throw her down to the floor.

"Fucking stay there."

She pulls at the cover on the bed to hold it against her ear.

"Fuck," I whisper, tired of this shit. I just want some damn answers, and depending on how they're answered, I'm out of here.

"Tell me why you're sleeping with my sister and this whore."

Roxy keeps her mouth shut… finally.

Jacob rubs his forehead, taking a deep breath.

"Roxy came to my office when there wasn't supposed to be anyone there and caught me walking without assistance. She threatened to rat me out to everyone, and that's when it began. She's always been jealous of Caoimhe, and having me in bed just boosted her ego. I didn't know what to do. I couldn't take the risk of my dad finding out. I had planned on making a recovery earlier, but now… I can't. He's sick, and I know he's dying. He hasn't said the words, but I can tell he's worse than what he's making out. Plus…" He stalls. "I didn't want to lose Caoimhe. I care for her, but after today, I doubt she'll give me a second chance."

Jacob looks defeated. I should feel sorry for him, but I don't. His dick didn't fall into Roxy, and he could have come clean with his dad, and why the hell not?

"Why? Why would you keep this from your dad?"

He looks at me with a scowl. "Do you not remember how demanding he is? How he expects more than one hundred percent of everything I do? Constantly comparing me to you. I just got sick of it. Being handicapped, he finally let up on me. Not demanding so much out of me. Not belittling me because I wasn't you. You have no idea because your family adores you."

He's wrong. My dad and I have had our issues as well, but I've never spoken about it to anyone and don't plan on starting now, especially with someone I haven't seen or talked to in years.

"Did you start the fire in my family's brewery?"

He shakes his head. "No, I was with Roxy that night. I found out when Caoimhe called me, upset."

I can tell he's telling the truth. The way his face falls from mentioning Caoimhe's name. He should have come clean. Sleeping with Roxy shouldn't have been a better option over caring what others thought of him.

I shake my head in disgust, looking between both of them. They belong together, but I have to remind myself this is Grace's half-brother. The thought leaves a bitter taste on my tongue. I hate that we will be bound together. I know my sister. Hatred for Jacob won't sit well when she finds out he's her half-brother. She's too innocent for her own good.

CHAPTER TWENTY-SIX

Mark

"Get your clothes on and get out."

I wait till Jacob wrestles about, getting his clothes. When he finishes gathering all his clothes but his shirt, he goes to Roxy and tries to pull it away from her hand.

Roxy has one hand on the bloody bed cover and the other holding on to the shirt with all her strength, fearful she may lose him once he walks out the door. Lose the future she's been desiring for years. She begins to plead with Jacob not to leave her.

"Please, Jacob, I only did it because you belong to me. Not her. ME! Why can't you see that? We're good together. So good."

He flinches at her words as if they were a sharp weapon assaulting him, cutting deep into his skin.

"No, we're not Roxy. I've tried being your friend. I've tried to understand why you're the way you are, but I didn't want to be anything other than a friend. Now... I don't even want that. I want you to leave and not bother me or Caoimhe again. Don't call me or come by, don't step foot near her, or I'll kill you myself."

Tears well up in her eyes.

"Fuck you!" she spits at him. "I loved you. I would have done anything for you. You'll see, you'll see that Caoimhe won't treat you like I did."

"You're not worth words, Roxy," Jacob says to her.

He yanks his shirt out of her grip and nods to me before he turns back around and goes to his wheelchair, sitting in it, he wheels himself over to the door. When he opens it, I warn him.

"Don't go near my sister," I say with a sneer without taking my eyes off Roxy.

I may not have harmed him, but it wasn't because I didn't want to. Grace is the only thing that will keep us from ripping each other apart.

Once I hear his retreat, I watch Roxy as she curls up into herself, the emotional pain too much for her. She begins to sob into her arms.

I don't feel anything. Not even a hint of sadness seeps in as her sobs fill the air. She's caused her pain.

"Don't you feel sorry for me?" she asks, looking down at the dirty carpet.

"Why would I?"

My words hit a nerve. She slowly raises her head, and I can see her hard eyes are dry and clear. She's clearly not upset.

A snarl forms on my lips, and my sight is blinded with rage. My hand rears back and flies forward, backhanding Roxy across the cheek.

Her body tumbles backward, hitting her head with a thud on the floor. A scream rips from her mouth so deafening, it pierces my eardrums with a sharp ring that makes me wince.

M'Aingeal is nothing like the piece of shit lying in front of me. Liz is pure innocence and would never try to con someone into getting something out of them.

Real tears begin slipping down her face, but no matter how many tears escape, they will never cleanse her wicked ways.

Roxy pulls herself together, then lifts herself up. She sits up against the bed, looking at me with a look of madness.

"Wow, you're such a man. Does it make you feel big to hit poor, defenseless women who don't have anything to defend themselves with? I bet your Liz thinks you're a catch." Her words are full of malice.

I tilt my head and draw close to her. She pushes her head back into the mattress, but it only gives so much before she can't move back any further.

"Don't ever say her name out of your filthy mouth again. You're nothing compared to her." My voice is low and heavy.

Roxy spits in my face, and an evil smile spreads across her face, and I can't help what I do next.

Standing up, I pull out the small hand pistol. Her face falls quickly, and the sickening smile she displayed seconds ago fades away like a lingering memory.

Aiming the pistol, I fire it, shooting Roxy in the forehead. One clear shot ends her sad, pathetic life. Pulling a handkerchief out of my back pocket, I wipe down the gun and throw it on the floor next to Roxy's limp body.

My cell rings, and I pull it out. Unknown caller scrolls across the screen. I push it to voicemail, then dial Sean.

"Mark." Sean's voice is cold.

"Sean, something wrong?"

"Only these idiots around here. They are worthless at times. What can I do you for?"

"I need a clean-up at The Green Pad, room two fifteen.

"Got it. I'll get someone on it."

I hang the phone up and walk out. When I make it downstairs to leave out the front door, I see the old lady behind the counter eyeing me, shaking her head. I know she had to hear the gunshot, and by the looks of this shit hole, I'm sure she sees and hears shit all the time.

When I open the front door, I'm met with a young group of

boys who are trying to pop open the door to the Audi.

"Fuck," I curse under my breath. "Get the fuck away," I yell at the young group as I walk to my car.

The skinny kid who's bent down trying to pop the lock looks up at the sound of my voice and scrambles away. The others follow suit. Just a reminder that this neighborhood is shit.

When I get on the highway my mind is racing if I should go to Liz before I speak to my sister. I need to tell Liz how I feel. How much I care for her and I'm just being protective.

CHAPTER TWENTY-SEVEN

Liz

I'm slumped up against the bathroom door when a bang startles me. My body jerks up, sitting straight, only to groan from the soreness in my neck. I rub it while trying to turn from left to right. *Shit, I'm sore.*

I don't know how I ended up asleep on the floor. I try to retrace the events that happened, but when a sudden crash occurs near the bathroom door, I lose my train of thought and stand up suddenly, making my head sway. Closing my eyes, I try to balance myself. The dizziness in my head doesn't subside, and I have to put a hand out to lean against the countertop, praying it will go away. The dizzy feeling turns into nausea, and I have to turn quickly to the toilet to relieve the contents that have crept up from my stomach.

Once I'm done heaving, I pull myself to the sink to wash up, groaning with each movement. The muscles in my stomach ache from the vomiting.

There's shouting and screaming in the hallway. Turning off the water to listen without interruption of the water, I hear Mark and Caoimhe arguing.

"I can do anything I fucking well please, Mark." Caoimhe's

voice bursts through the walls like a hammer.

"Why the hell would you want to be with someone like him."

"If you must know —"

"Don't fucking say it. I can tell by the look on your face it's not his bank account you're into."

Standing within an inch of the door, I can hear Mark's heavy breathing as Caoimhe's footsteps storm off in the distance.

"Then don't fucking ask me."

Slam.

The door opens and crashes into the wall when Caoimhe yells out, "You don't have a clue as to what has changed around here. So, if you don't want to hear it, go back to your perfect little world in New York, Brother."

Slam.

I can feel Mark's anger seeping through the walls, stifling the air with bitterness.

Crash.

I let out a high-pitched scream when Mark's fist crashes through the thick wood door.

"What the fuck!" Mark yells.

Pulling back his fist, he tries to open the doorknob, but it's locked. My mind is a mess, and I was hoping to get out of here before he came back.

"Liz… are you okay? Open the door, Baby," he says in a soothing voice.

Baby?

My brows scrunch together. He's never called me anything but *M'Aingeal.* Could he know? How could he find out? I haven't said anything to anyone about leaving.

I look over at my suitcase and quickly set it in the corner of the glass-enclosed shower, hoping it'll be out of sight enough that he won't be able to see it.

When I open the door, Mark stands right in front of me with a painful expression in his eyes. He passes me to go to the sink, where he turns the water on and places his hand under the running water.

"What are you doing in here? Is there something wrong with our bathroom?"

Mark's questions make my heart rate pick up. I hate lying, but if I want to get away, I have to.

"The toilet wasn't working, so… I came in here."

He looks up, burning me with his gaze. I can tell he's not sure to believe me.

"Here, let me help."

Taking hold of his hand, I hold it under the faucet while the water cascades over it, washing the blood away like a fading memory.

His penetrating gaze never leaves me, making me uneasy.

"What was all that about?" I ask, trying to kill the silence that has filled the room.

"Nothing."

"It didn't sound like nothing." Our eyes meet, and there's something in his gaze that makes it hard to look away.

His beautiful ambers are bright with a softness that I haven't seen before.

Did that fight with Caoimhe cause Mark pain?

I rest my hand on the side of his face, wanting to pull out any negative energy that is causing him discomfort. He closes his eyes and leans into my touch. Pressing myself closer to him, I bring my lips to his and kiss him softly.

There's no need for this moment to be rushed, and it's perfect. It's the kiss I waited my whole teenage life for. When we break from one another, it takes me a moment to come down from the high.

"Oh, here, let me get you a towel or something to wrap your hand."

I start opening the cabinets, searching for anything to use. When I open the bottom cabinet, I notice a first aid kit, and I grab it and sit it on the counter. When I look in the mirror at Mark, I see his eyes set on something. What they're locked on has my heart pounding.

"Were you planning on going somewhere without telling me?"

There's hurt in his voice—nothing like what I expected. I expected him to be cruel, like the normal man I've grown accustomed to.

I open my mouth to respond, but my voice escapes me, leaving me wondering how I am going to find the words to tell Mark I was going to leave. Instead, I cast my eyes down to look at my shoes.

Regret washes over me in a tsunami wave, making me want to take back my plan of leaving. I can tell Mark has more than what he bargained for when he came home. Pain is etched into every crinkle on his face, and it makes my heart break for him. Break for all the secrets kept within the walls of this luxurious manor.

Betrayal runs deep in the soil of his family land. I know all too well about being betrayed by loved ones. My loveless life brought me to be a slave in a criminal world that I've desperately tried to run away from, only to be drugged back into the arms of a man who owns my body and consumes my soul.

"Answer me, Liz. Were you planning on leaving?"

I slowly nod without making eye contact.

Why am I suddenly afraid of hurting Mark? After all he's done, I shouldn't care, but for some reason that is strange to me, I do.

"I don't—"

"Stop."

My eyes flash back up to Mark.

"Don't go." His face is laced with pain.

"Tell me why I shouldn't?"

He wraps his uninjured arm around my waist to pull me flush against his body.

"Because you're the only thing that makes sense in my life, and I don't want to lose you."

I'm speechless. His words of affection don't belong being spoken from his beautiful lips. They're foreign from his corrupted ways.

I swallow. I want him, that is undeniable, but his ways and his lifestyle are something I don't want in my life.

"Mark... I can't stay. I—"

His lips crash against mine, and I feel my resistance crumbling beneath my feet. When I don't fight against the pull, I open my mouth to allow our tongues to dance together. When Mark ends our moment of tenderness, his nose brushes against mine.

"I need you," he whispers.

That's it. That's all it takes for me to give him a nod. To give him access to my heart. One of the most dangerous men I've ever known *needing me* sends my heart falling into a dark pit that I know I'll lose my soul in.

With my heart in hand, I finally tell Mark what I want.

"I want a better life. I want one that doesn't involve criminals and acts of injustice. I don't have to have the white picket fence. I just want... normal."

He nods, and I don't know if he is agreeing to give me the life I've hoped and dreamed of all my life or if he understands I need to seek out what I want elsewhere.

"Speak to me, Mark. Tell me if I should look for that elsewhere."

His ambers are full of hope. Hope that I'm going to stay.

"I can't promise anything. This is who I am. My dark world began long before you and will always live dormant within me, but I can give you a life filled with love because I do love you."

I close my eyes and let his words soak into my skin, seeping deep into my heart.

CHAPTER TWENTY-EIGHT

Mark

Liz has my cold black heart twisted, bleeding me of any sin running through my veins. She makes me want to be a better man, but can I? Can I be the man she deserves? Give her a life without having tainted hands? This desire I have to take souls from this world they destroy with their selfish and cruel ways is embedded in me, but I can't lose her. She gives me a reason to want to make a house become a home and to change the man I have become.

Liz opens her eyes and takes in a large breath of air. I can see the doubt swirling around in her mind. She's trying to decide if she can trust my words.

"One chance." Her words bite into my skin, reminding me I'm not good enough for a woman like her. "You have one chance to show me you're going to be true to your word that you'll try to change."

A smile stretches across my face, but I know I don't deserve her. She should be running away from me, not wanting anything to do with me, but a calmness I've never felt envelops me with hope that I can come close to the man she wants in her life.

"Baby steps, okay?" I need to make certain she knows I need time to make a lifestyle change. I need time to wrap up loose ends and put things in place before I can make an honest living or come as close to being honest as I can.

"Baby steps, but Mark, I won't stay if you continue, and you won't find me next time I leave town." Her words are filled with promises that I know she will live up to.

I grin. "Yes, ma'am." I lean into her ear, dusting my hand over her breast. Softly taking her hand, I place it on my arse. "I'll let you take it out on this if I get out of line."

When I pull back, she gives me a lopsided look, amusement dancing in her eyes. I've never, not once, been playful with Liz. That's a side of me I only show to Wilder and Blaze. I demand respect from the men who work under me, and I know I've messed up and have shown Liz the same side.

A scream rips through the air, breaking the playfulness Liz and I had.

Without a second thought, I draw out my gun and instruct Liz to stay. Closing the door, I rush from the bathroom to the sound down the hallway. The screams coming from Caoimhe's room.

Kicking the door open, another scream echoes through the room, barely audible to my ears from the sound of wood being split.

Stepping inside, I expect to see Caoimhe in danger. Instead, she's sitting on her bed with a vice grip on her cell, screaming into the phone.

Walking to her, I take the phone away. "Who is this?" There's no answer. Pulling the phone back, I look at the screen. The fucker hung up.

"Who were you talking to?"

Caoimhe's eyes are filled with tears. Her lips tremble as she tries to tell me who it was.

"Jacob." She says in a low, shaky tone.

My nostrils flare, angry he went against my words and called her.

"Did he call you?"

She shakes her head.

"Why are you calling him?"

"More importantly, what did you do to Roxy?"

My eyes turn into slits. Why would she care what I did to Roxy? Wasn't Roxy betraying her?

"Caoimhe," I say her name firmly. She's not to question me. I did what I needed to do because Roxy was trouble, and she wouldn't have stopped even if she had wed Jacob. She would make sure all of our lives were a living hell. "Did you start that fire at the brewery?"

She gasps as if offended by my question.

"NO! You should know better than to ask me that question." She pauses, giving me an evil eye. "Maybe you should be questioning a young certain someone you think is too innocent to do anything wrong." She looks over my shoulder and continues. "Don't question my loyalty to this family, Mark. I've been here the whole time. I've been the one left to pick up the pieces while you were off doing whatever you wanted. I've kept Mum from losing her mind when Dad got hurt in the fire. Me, Mark. Me."

Have I been so selfish that I haven't considered what my sisters have been going through? My dad is a man who is driven. While he loves his family, he won't let his work go to the side to have dinner with his wife and kids. He always missed birthdays and special holidays. He only came along for family vacations because Mum made him, but he always worked.

I walk over to the side of the bed and sit beside Caoimhe, pulling her to my chest. She's so much like my Mum—small frame, dark features, and long dark hair with slight waves. She's as beautiful as my mum, too.

"I'm sorry, Caoimhe." I kiss her temple. "I should have come back before now." I pull back to get a better look at her face. Hooking a finger under her chin, I catch a tear as it tries to roll off. "Things are going to change. I've changed. Coming home is something I should've done years ago." I let her absorb my words. "Why were you talking to Jacob, and what did you mean asking someone who seems so innocent?" I know who she's referring to, Grace, but I want to hear Caoimhe say her name to confirm my suspicions.

Grace would be the last one that anyone would suspect. She's the baby of the family, a college student, and she and Dad have a close relationship, but it wouldn't make sense for her to hurt him. Unless… she found out she's not his, but still, he doesn't even know she's not his.

Caoimhe eyes cast down. "I wanted to talk to Jacob about us, but he ended it."

"Finish. Who are you talking about that's not so innocent?"

"Never mind, it doesn't matter."

With my finger still hooked under her chin, I lift her face. "It matters to me."

Her cell rings in her hand. I cast my eyes down to see who the caller is, and I notice it's fucking Jacob again.

Caoimhe looks at me before she answers.

"Yes." There's a brief silence before a tear rolls down her face. "I'll let everyone know, and we're on our way."

When she clicks the end button, I wait for her to tell me what his call was about.

"Mr. Hallmark has taken a turn for the worse, and the doctor is there with him. They don't think he has much time left. I hate that Dad is still not responsive. I know they have been so close. He'd want to be there to see him take his last breath."

I nod. A movement at the door catches my eye. *M'Aingeal* is standing at the doorway with a look of shock, her face pale.

Something is wrong.

"Let's go. We can tell the others when we head out." I stand waiting for Caoimhe.

"You go ahead. I'm going to freshen up."

When she sees my facial expressions, she says, "So I can rub it in his face that I'm way hotter than Roxy has ever been. Nothing more."

I smile. There's the badass I know.

***

Liz and I leave ahead of everyone. When we arrive at the Hallmarks, only a few cars are parked outside the large house that looks more like a castle. Mrs. Hallmark always had expensive taste and wanted everyone to know they had money.

When I get out, I walk over to Liz. She's already standing outside the door. Reaching for her hand, she meets me halfway and interlaces her fingers with mine. It's not forced. It's welcoming me into her world, body and soul. There's a proud feeling in my chest. This beautiful, sweet, and smart woman is mine. I'm the only man who knows every freckle, dimple, and curve of her body.

We walk hand in hand to the front door, and before I can ring the doorbell, it opens with Jacob standing there.

"Thanks for coming," he says weakly.

I give him a nod, and we walk inside. I make eye contact with Liz, and I can tell she's surprised to see Jacob out of his wheelchair. I don't address it. The last thing I want is to talk about Jacob with my woman.

My woman. The sound is foreign to my thoughts. I knew Liz was mine, but my woman is something different. It's a promise to love her, to keep her safe, and to do my best to be better for her.

"Is he upstairs?"

"Yeah, you remember his room. He's not going to make it through the night. I can stay behind with Liz if you want to visit him."

I almost laugh. If he thinks I trust him to be with my woman, he's fucked in the head more than I thought.

"No." With our hands still interlaced, I pull Liz to the grand staircase. "Liz is going with me." We head up the stairs, hands laced and souls bound to one another. Before we get to Mr. Hallmark's double bedroom doors, Liz stops me out of view from prying eyes below.

"What the hell is going on? He was just in a wheelchair like yesterday."

"M'Aingeal." I tuck her long, blonde hair behind her ear. "It's a long story."

She raises an eyebrow, waiting for me to tell her.

"Not here. I'll tell you another time. Right now, I want to show my respects to Mr. Hallmark, then we'll go."

She inhales and releases the air she was holding. "Okay, but remember"—she grabs my arse—"it's mine if you don't talk."

I smile and wrap my arm around her. Pulling her into my body, I grind my semi-hard cock into her center. Growing harder, I say, "If you do that again, I'll take you into the bathroom and fuck you so hard, you'll wake the dead."

Her eyes widen. I bend down to bite her neck, startling her. She bucks forward, making me growl from the pressure she pushes on my cock.

"Behave," she warns.

CHAPTER TWENTY-NINE

Mark

My heart is pounding in my hand, wanting to escape through my fingertips only to land at Liz's mercy. How did I get to this point? The point of being lovesick. I shake my head. Somewhere along the dark and rough road, this woman has branded herself deep into my bloodstream.

Liz squeezes my hand, bringing me out of my thoughts.

"Mark," Mr. Hallmark's voice is a whisper.

Leaving Liz standing close to the door, I walk to his side. Bending down on my knee, I take in John's frail appearance. He's lost more weight since I saw him last. His sickness has taken its toll on his body, making him look nothing like the man he used to be.

I don't care for him, but I won't deny he once meant something to our family. Our families were always together during the holidays, taking vacations when we were young. I clench my jaw, thinking about how close he and my mum became.

"John," I say his name with disdain, trying to rein in my emotions of his betrayal of my father.

"I need," he coughs. "I need you to promise me something,"

he coughs again, and this time, blood drips from his nose.

Grabbing a tissue, I pass it to him.

His hand shakes as he reaches for it.

"I need you to give me your word you'll tell Grace that Jacob is her brother. I don't want Jacob to be alone. He's always been a bit... much, but he needs family."

John knows if I give him my word, I will stand by it. The problem is that I don't want to give my word. I don't want to be the one to tell Grace that all she's known her whole life is a lie. My mum should be the one he should ask, not me.

Their actions have caused a heavy cloud to fog the direction we'll all be taking in the future. Because of their disloyalty to their spouses, we're left dealing with the repercussions. So, instead of answering, I choose to ignore it. I can't give him something I'm not willing to accept—an affair that led to my sister.

"John, you need to rest. Save your strength."

As I stand and pull the cover up his fragile body, his nurse comes in the room, letting us know visiting time is over.

"Wait," John pleads. "You haven't given your word."

Fuck. Why me? Why is he asking me to do this?

"I can see the turmoil in your expression," he coughs again, and the nurse comes over to usher us out, but John stops her. "You have to understand, we didn't want to hurt anyone."

My teeth grind together. *Hurt anyone.* He laid down with my mum, his best friend's wife, and he says he didn't want to hurt anyone.

Soft, delicate hands wrap around my arm, and I feel the tension ease away. Liz's touch has always brought inner peace to the beast inside me. Placing my hand on top of hers, I try to pull us toward the bedroom door. I need to leave before I say something that will haunt me. Lashing out at a dying man will leave scars that not even God himself would forgive.

Liz doesn't move. Instead, she stays with her feet planted.

Our eyes meet, and I can see what she wants. She wants me to give my word, but instead, I look back to John and nod. It's not words, but it's good enough for him to know I'll do as he asks.

Once we leave the room, we're met with more voices echoing from downstairs. My family must be here. It grates my nerves that Mum came. Did she come to wish her dying lover goodbye?

Liz's hands tug my arm, and we stop at the top of the staircase.

"What was that? Grace is Jacob's sister?"

My chest heaves. I can't do this. I can't answer questions and deal with having to tell Grace. I'm pissed that Mum had an affair, and now my father is in a coma, and we don't know when he will wake up.

Laughter bounces off the walls lined with pictures of a husband, wife, and son that are more of a sham than an actual family. It makes me wonder if our walls are lined with the same deceitfulness.

"Let's go."

It's the only words I can chew out. I need to get my head straight and my words if I'm going to be forced to keep my word, and I always keep my word.

When we reach the bottom of the staircase, I see all my sisters and Mum sitting in the formal living room with Jacob. Something about the scene flips my stomach.

Grace sits beside Jacob with her hand on his back, running in circles. It's not a lingering touch. No, it's to comfort him.

Does she know? Could she be aware he's her half-brother?

When my eyes flash to my Mum, I'm met with hers, and I can tell she's been crying.

My face hardens, my eyebrows draw in, and I hear Liz whimper at my side, waking me out of the haze of hatred I feel for the weakness my mum had with another man.

My grip on Liz's hand is too tight. I must rein in my

emotions. I know she sees it. Mum's eyes quickly break with my stare.

"Mum," I wait for her to respond.

She will be the one to break the news to Grace. I won't be the bad guy here. It's her mistake. She's at fault for causing this between our families. She and the dying man upstairs.

When she meets my eyes, I tilt my head toward the library. I need to make sure she understands this is her doing and she will be the one to tell this story.

"Liz, go have a seat. I need to speak to Mum." The word Mum tastes sour on my tongue. Never has that word ever affected me other than as an endearment.

Liz's eyes search mine, looking for direction. Leaning into the only woman who has captured my dark heart, I slide my hand into her hair and bend down to take her lips in a kiss that I want to lose myself in.

Breaking our kiss, I say softly, "I need to take care of some personal matters. It won't take long."

I can tell she wants to say something. Instead, she walks over to the couch where Caoimhe is seated, looking at Grace with a death stare. Caoimhe doesn't know. She doesn't know that Jacob's blood runs through Grace, too.

Making our way into the library, I shut the door behind Mum. I don't even wait for her to sit before I start. The last thing I came in here to do is to get comfortable. I need to get this shit show over. I'm ready to go home.

"You need to tell Grace now."

Her chest deflates. She's been putting this off for way too long.

"John has asked for me to tell her. He wants Jacob to know they're half-siblings." I bite my tongue, waiting for her to respond, doing my best to be patient because patience is something I have little of.

"I knew this day would come. I just... was hoping it

wouldn't," she says as if she's still unsure if she wants to tell Grace.

Opening the door, I call out for Grace to meet up in the library.

As she gets up, I follow Caoimhe's eyesight as her eyes never leave Grace's back. *Fuck!*

This couldn't get more complicated. The last thing this family needs is more secrets and distaste for one another. As much as I hate the fact Grace is Jacob's half-sibling, it needs to be out in the open. Grace doesn't need to have feelings for Jacob other than a sibling.

Grace walks in and immediately sits beside Mum, reaching out for her hands.

"What is it?"

Grace doesn't look surprised about us asking her in here. She doesn't even look concerned. Her face is relaxed. There's no tension in her body as to why she's here. Could she know?

Mum opens her mouth and looks at me, but I give her a shake of my head. She's asking me to start this, and she's the one I want to own up to what she has done to our family.

"Grace," she pauses. "Grace, years ago, your dad was always working to build the brewery to what it is today. I got lonely. Sure, I had your brother and sisters, but it's different from having a spouse to show you love and affection. It's a different kind of companionship than you have with your children. I'm not trying to justify what I did. I just want you to understand a little more. Your dad and I weren't speaking or even seeing much of each other during the time you were conceived." She stops and looks into Grace's eyes, hoping she'll understand without having to say it.

Grace's body language doesn't give away what she's feeling or if she is even following where Mum is going with this story.

"Go on, Mum. Finish the story," I say, a little too harshly, wanting her to just come out with it.

Inhaling air, she says, "During that time, John was coming out to the manor to check on me, and while the kids were at sporting events or with friends, we were growing closer than we should have. I realized that after it happened. I shouldn't have let it get that far, but I was lonely, and the attention he was showing me felt so good. During the time of our passionate affair, you were conceived."

We both look, waiting for Grace to register what was just told to her. There's nothing, not even a blink.

Grace pulls her hands away, sits back on the small settee, and crosses her legs.

"I've been waiting for you to tell me."

Flashes of what Caoimhe said: *Maybe you should be questioning a young certain someone you think is too innocent to do anything wrong.* I finally understand Caoimhe's words. I may not be the only other black sheep in this fucked-up family. Maybe this dark side that has always had more power over my life comes from my mum.

"How?" Mum gasps, as if she can't believe Grace already knew. "No one knew." She fumbles with the hem of her shirt. "Not even your father knows."

"Really?" Grace says sarcastically. "Do you think he doesn't realize I look nothing like his other daughters or son? I have your eyes and that man upstairs' bone structure. I found out when I found my birth certificate, which you have kept from me all my life. Hiding it so I couldn't get to it when I asked because I needed it for my school."

Mum stands with a stiff back resembling a rod rammed down it.

"Do not talk to me in that tone, Grace Hope. I'm still your mum. Your father loves you, and I couldn't do that to him. I couldn't tell him you were John's daughter. Do you think his evil wife would have allowed you to be close to him or Jacob? That woman only cared about appearances. She was my friend, but I knew the real woman under those designer clothes.

"I'm sorry you're just now hearing this from me, but John is dying, and Jacob needs you. I know I should've said something, but I couldn't. I didn't want to ruin your relationship with your father—the only man who has loved you from day one.

"John knew you were his, and he chose not to take responsibility. He knew how his wife would react, and he didn't want to lose his fortune. What does that say about a man? That he cared more about his wife's money than he did about his child."

Mum starts to cry. Pushing myself off the edge of the desk, I walk over and pull her to my chest, stroking her hair to ease her nerves. While I disagree with how poorly she has handled this, I don't want to see her in pain.

A look of regret rests on Grace's face.

If anything, I know our family has always been close. Today is no different. We feel each other's pain. Just as I feel Caoimhe's pain of what Jacob did to her and may have never gotten too close to a woman for them to hurt me, I can relate to wanting to get back at the pain someone caused me.

CHAPTER THIRTY

Mark

Grace comes over to wrap her arms around our Mum.

"Don't cry," Grace's words are filled with sorrow. "I'm sorry. I wish you would have told me sooner. I've waited for years for you to tell me. I even threw hints that I wanted you to say something only to be ignored."

Mum peels herself off of my chest, and her tears are left behind, soaked into my shirt like a bad memory.

"I haven't even told your father. How was I supposed to tell you? I couldn't bear the thought of hurting the only man I have ever loved. He loves you. I didn't think it was hurting anyone. John wasn't interested in being a part of your life. He only wanted Jacob because it tied him to his wife's family money. I wanted to protect you. Protect your feelings. I know it was selfish of me, and for that, I'm sorry, but I did what I thought was best."

"It's time you tell our father. It's time for all of this to be behind us so we can move on and be the family I once thought we were," I tell her with authority.

I'm the man of the house since my father cannot be in charge. My father. The one man I have known my entire life has always been a man of honor. I want to laugh at the scenario playing out in front of me—Mum having an affair with his best friend. A dishonesty that runs so deep between them, it's created another life—Grace.

My phone vibrates in my pocket, letting me know I have an incoming message. When I pull it out of my pocket, it's a message from the alarm system I had installed at the manor. In all the years my parents have lived there, they have never considered their safety.

Why would they? They live simple lives, and knowing everyone in the community helps. Everyone looks out for one another, and it feels like a safety net. Not the world I live in where danger seeks you out, looking to destroy anything and everything you love or own. That's the reason I've chosen to keep Liz hidden, not to speak of her or to show her how I truly feel. I wanted to keep her safe.

My muscles tense with the thought of bringing Liz back to New York. Knowing someone could hurt *M'Aingeal* to come after me has my blood running cold, causing my body to feel numb. I have always welcomed the numbness that flows through my veins. It allows me not to feel for people. Not to care about them or anyone close to them. It's how I'm so good at my job. But now, I'm concerned for the woman who holds my heart.

Taking a long breath of air to release the tension building, I switch on the app for the security system I had installed a few days ago. I don't see anything unusual, but I need to check to ensure it's nothing.

Today has been the only day no one has been with my father. Aine left the house when I arrived home, and I was too focused on wanting to speak to Caoimhe to call anyone to stay with him. He should be fine, but whoever burned down our business could be in the manor.

My sisters, Ciara and Clodagh, were supposed to take their

turn staying with him, but as much as I love them, they don't have a caregiver bone in their body. Being young as they are, they tend to only care about their own needs.

"Stay here. Don't come home until I tell you to." My Mum wants to argue, but I put my finger up for her to wait. "I'll call you. I've got a notification from the security app that there's movement in the house, and we still don't know who started that fire at the brewery."

I look over at Grace to watch her reaction to my words, but she still gives nothing away. Right now, I need to check on the house, but I will discuss it with her.

Pocketing my phone, I ease out of the library and almost make it to the front door before Liz calls my name. Not waiting, I open the door.

"Mark." She's walking quickly to catch up with me. "Wait, damn it!"

Turning to her, I say, "Liz, stay here till I return."

"Where are you going?" she asks with a softness that gives away her concerns.

I'm not used to having to answer to someone. This relationship is new and something I want more than the air I breathe, but it will take some getting used to.

"There's movement on the security camera at the manor. I'll be back, *M'Aingeal*," Reaching down to tilt her chin up, I look at her angelic face. She's beautiful. I've known inside of me from the moment I saw her, she would only ever be mine.

She nods in understanding, and I kiss her full lips, hating to have to pull away to leave. Shutting the door, I leave my angel inside, safe until I return.

***

Fifteen minutes later, I arrive at the manor. Cutting off the car and making sure not to slam the door shut, I pull out my gun and head around the back. I want to make sure all the doors and windows are secure or to see where the intruder made their way in.

After inspecting the outside, there doesn't appear to be any broken windows or doors. Reaching for the back doorknob, I twist it only to find it's locked.

I find that odd. How did anyone get into the house if it's locked up?

Pulling out my house key, I slowly unlock the door and push it open, aiming my Glock in front of me, ready to fire at anything that moves. I won't think twice before I pull the trigger, so this mother fucker better hope he's prayed up.

The kitchen is empty, as expected. I tread lightly through the first floor, checking out all the rooms. Nothing. When I come to my father's study, I hear a noise. It's a song that has been burned into my mind from a young age, and I only know one person who listens to that old folk song. My father.

I shove the door with force and aim my gun at the one person I didn't expect to be standing in front of me, smoking a damn cigar.

CHAPTER THIRTY-ONE

Mark

"What the fuck are you doing here?"

Blaze jumps, sending his cigar flying in the air and landing on the other side of the room.

"Fucking hell. You scared the shit out of me. Why did you do that?"

I shake my head at him. How did this arse get into the house?

"What the hell are you doing here?"

"I'm here to collect your arse." He gets up from my father's desk and goes to retrieve his cigar. "Work is piling up, and you're wanted."

I never told anyone why I left. I didn't expect to be here this long.

"How did you get into the house?" I ask, ignoring him.

"I came through the front door arsehole." When he picks up the cigar, it's broken. "Fuck," he says under his breath.

I tilt my head to the small bar beside him. "Pour me a whiskey." Putting my gun back into the holster, I sit in front of the desk, rubbing the tension out of my face. "It's been a day," I say to no one.

Blaze sets my whiskey on the table and walks behind the desk, taking a seat in the oversized brown leather chair.

"I heard about your dad." He pulls out another cigar, preparing it to light it up.

Not speaking, I take a drink of the whiskey and welcome the burn when it slides down my throat. I've always loved that feeling. I guess I'm just a little fucked up in a way that pain can bring me so much calmness.

"I don't have to guess who told you?" I raise an eyebrow.

After inhaling a drag off the cigar, his eyes close as he releases the intoxicating taste of the cigar through his nostrils.

"Sean."

It figures. One thing about Sean is that he loves to tell other people's shit. That's the reason why we keep in touch with him. He's a reliable source for knowing any dirty details on a person who may be trying to do business with us.

For a few minutes, we sit in silence. I can't help but think about the fire at the brewery. The police report was finally available for me to pick up, and the listing on the cause of the fire was a bad breaker in the power panel. How did that happen? Everything was new except for one circuit breaker.

A loud noise occurs on the second floor right above the study, making me and Blaze both turn our heads to look at the ceiling.

When the sound doesn't occur again, we look back at each other. Words are not needed. We both draw our guns. Walking as lightly as a two-hundred-and-fifty-pound man can, we creep out of the study to head upstairs to investigate.

When my feet touch the second floor, I hear scuffling down the hall in my parent's bedroom. I signal to Blaze to follow me. When we step in front of the bedroom door, the floor pops.

I cringe, knowing whoever is on the other side heard the floor. Reaching my hand out, I push open the door. I don't know what I'm expecting, but I'm ready for whatever shit is about to go down.

When the door swings wide, I take a giant step into the master bedroom, gun pointed, ready to take someone out. Nothing. I put my finger up to my mouth and then point down to the floor, letting Blaze know to be quiet and stay put while I search the room.

After searching the room, coming up empty-handed, I put my gun back into my holster on my back hip.

"Fucking hell," Blaze comments.

"Yeah, I know I didn't just hear whatever that noise was," I say, studying the room.

There's nothing out of place. Not a single item on the floor to give away if someone knocked something off the dresser, but when I study my dad lying on the bed, I notice something so out of place, my eyes don't believe I'm seeing it.

"Meet me downstairs," I whisper to Blaze.

He gives me a head tip and walks out, leaving me and my dad in the room alone.

"It's the first time we've been alone, old man," I say out loud, making sure I can be heard.

I walk over to the side of the bed where my father is lying, dragging a chair with me. I place it by the bed, sit, and cross my ankle over my knee.

Taking in a long breath of air, I feel defeated. I've thought long and hard about why there was only one breaker that was old and out of place in a new electric panel. I checked the papers in the office cabinet and found an invoice from a company that came out and installed a brand-new electric panel. The same one that had the old breaker. There's only one explanation.

"It was a sham, wasn't it?" Crossing my arms, I wait.

My father lies still. The only movement is the rise and fall of his chest. Uncrossing my leg, I lean forward, placing my elbows on my knees.

"You pleading the fifth?"

I'm second-guessing myself. Maybe he was lying on this side of the bed, and my mind was playing tricks on me. I bow my head, shaking it, "Fuck, I don't know what I'm doing."

Standing up, I take one last look at my father, then turn to head downstairs until I feel a burning feeling at the back of my head. Turning on my toes, I catch what I've known all along.

"Open your eyes. I know you're not in a fucking coma."

His eyes are shut, but they're flicking like he's trying to decide if he wants to open them.

Standing on the spot where I turned around, I wait. I'm not moving until his eyes open to face the deception he's portrayed.

Lazily, he peels his eyelids open. His dark brown irises hold a stand-off with my amber ones. Neither one of us speaks. There's only the heavy, suffocating presence of his sham filling in the space all around us.

"How did you know?" he asks in his deep voice.

My teeth grind so hard, I feel certain I've cracked my back molars.

"You forget I'm good at looking into things. The more important question is, why did you do it? Why put up this sham and ruin everything you worked so hard for?" My voice rises. "Do you realize how much that brewery took away from our family? You destroyed it with a flick of a match." A shocking revelation occurs to me. "You know, don't you?" It's a simple question, one that doesn't require much thought for him to answer.

He gives me a settled nod, then throws the cover off. His legs have faint burn marks but nothing that requires surgery. Rising out of the bed, he stands a little shorter than me. Old age has drawn him over slightly.

We look into each other's eyes, and I can feel the emotions he's hiding behind him. There's resentment, regret, and something that looks like hope.

"Grace came to the office asking questions I wasn't quite understanding. When she stormed off to her car, I followed her but didn't get to stop her in time before she drove off. Her birth certificate blew up from the ground, slapping me in the face." He laughs, and it sounds forced. "Can you imagine? It was like a bad omen punching me in the face for working hard to provide a good life for my family." He runs his hands up his face. "My best fucking friend," he says as he tugs his hair, trying to pull out what he's got gripped in his hands.

"Doesn't give you the right to burn down the brewery. Why did you do it?"

He drops on the bed, staring straight at the wall, willing it to swallow him whole. Shrugging his shoulder, he continues.

"I don't care about anything as much as I care about your mum. I... guess I thought I would burn it down, hoping to burn the past along with it. Only when I woke up in the hospital, I felt more shameful."

There's a tapping noise behind me, and I smell the familiar scent of lavender. Looking over my shoulder, my whole family is observing us like a bunch of damn spectators waiting for a brawl. He's not seen them yet because he continues speaking.

"You see, son, I already threw you to the side. It broke me when I did that. Then I found out Grace wasn't mine but my best friend's. I was upset at everyone—your Mum, John, but mainly myself—for not being there for your mum when she needed my attention the most." His eyes fill with tears. "I'm sorry for what I did all those years ago. After I said those words, I felt awful about it. I came home as soon as possible, but you had already left. I searched your room and saw all the drawers open. Your clothes were missing, and I knew I was too late. I didn't know where to look for you, or maybe I was a coward for not trying harder. I hope you can forgive me." He looks at me with pleading eyes.

Expressing myself through words has never been easy for me. I do the only thing I've always been known to do and walk away, leaving him to work out his problems with my mum, who is standing by Liz.

Reaching out to grasp Liz's hand, I lead her to our room.

CHAPTER THIRTY-TWO

Liz

I wake up to a large, calloused hand squeezing my knee.

"M'Aingeal, we're home," Mark's lips brush my forehead, laying a kiss before they leave my skin.

Blinking my eyes several times, I try to remember where I am.

After Mark stormed back to our bedroom with me in tow, he gathered his clothes and threw them in his bag without a word. When we left the manor, he told me that he needed to get back to work, that some things needed his attention.

I've debated asking Mark if he's touched base with his family, but I think better of it. I don't want to get into his family's mess. I know, right now, his dad and mom need time to talk and heal from the secrets that have been kept.

I force myself to rise out of the white leather seat. It's been a long flight, and I'm desperately wanting to get home to my bed.

After a good rest, I plan on going to work. I left without a word to my boss. When I landed in Ireland, I texted him that I had an emergency to attend to out of town. He was kind enough to understand and tell me to take as much time as I needed.

Mark waits for me at the door of the private plane with a warm smile. My heart skips at the site of this large man displaying a smile for me.

The small amount of gray he has in his beard and hair shines from the sun bouncing into the plane. Perfect straight white teeth and a handsome face, along with his large frame, is a sight that could make any woman melt into a puddle.

But it's Mark's softer side I'm falling hard for. The way he expressed that he needed me sent my heart into a spiral of affection. Never has anyone said those words to me. *They needed me.* I've always felt that I wasn't needed by anyone. That I could disappear tomorrow, and no one would even know I existed except for the birth certificate I'd leave behind.

Walking past Mark, he puts his hand on the small of my back to lead us to a black Lincoln waiting for us.

"When we get back to my penthouse, I want you naked and sitting on my face. I want your taste on my tongue for the rest of the night."

His words about when we get back to his house make me halt. Mark slams into my back, almost knocking me over. If it wasn't for his hand reaching out to wrap around my waist, I would have face-planted on the asphalt.

Turning on my heel, I say, "Mark, I have a job to return to. A house to return to."

His face contorts with anger. "You're mine. Your things are placed in my house, where you belong." His finger points at me.

I almost shrink in size from my shoulders deflating.

"You're never going to change, are you?" I whisper. Tears burn the back of my eyes.

His eyes soften, and his large hands cup my face.

"*M'Aingeal*, my beautiful angel. I can't make sure you're safe if you're not with me... I love you." He kisses my forehead, leaving his lingering lips there while my heart melts at the sincerity of his words.

He uses his large hands to move into my hair, and I wrap my arms around his neck to pull him to me. My lips crash into his, and I push my tongue into his mouth, seeking out his. I want this moment to last forever. Never have three words meant more to me than hearing he loves me. Only my grandmother had ever said she loved me.

Our kiss is interrupted when Blaze starts yelling, "Hey, do I get this show for free, or do I need to buy a ticket."

Mark growls, breaking our kiss.

I laugh at the banter these two men have going on between them.

"Fucker, get your arse in the car," Mark tells Blaze, who's currently hanging out of the sunroof of the black Lincoln.

Pointing my finger at Mark, I say, "We're not done talking about this."

Mark grunts, adjusting himself.

The way back to Mark's has me in a ball of nerves. There's something about being back in New York that has me on edge. Memories float around me, making me feel that I'm being watched.

Maybe it's Carla's ghost.

Maybe she's warning me of danger yet to come.

Whatever it is has the hairs on my arms standing up.

When we pull up to an apartment building I used to pass every day on my way to school, I'm surprised.

"You didn't realize I lived in this building?" Mark asks.

I'm shaking my head because the apartments in this building are more than what I could afford. My month's salary wouldn't be able to cover a month's rent.

When the car stops in front of the double glass doors of the apartment complex, Mark opens the door, telling Blaze he'll be at Club Red tonight.

Grabbing our bags, he leads the way through the doors. I follow him, taking in the floor's décor and the overpriced artwork hanging in the lobby.

"The way you've got your mouth open will come to good use when we get inside my apartment. I'm going to fill it with my cock."

"Mark," I hiss. My eyes move about the lobby to make sure no one heard him.

He laughs again, and I decide it's my new favorite sound.

When we enter the elevator and the doors close, Mark's hand reaches into my hair, pulling my head back. His tongue darts out to lick his bottom lip, tucking it back into his mouth.

"You think I was playing when I said I was going to fill that mouth with my cock?" He raises an eyebrow, waiting for me to answer him.

Instead, I wrap my fingers around the top of his jeans and unfasten them, bringing the zipper down. His manhood springs out. Wrapping my hands around his large girth, I stroke him.

His eyes close, and he moans.

"You're going to be a good little girl and suck me off, aren't you?"

I don't get to answer before he pushes me down onto my knees, using the firm grip that he has on my hair for leverage. His other hand grabs the base of his cock.

"Stick out your tongue."

Sticking out my tongue, he places the tip on it. Slapping my tongue with his cock a few times, he then thrusts into my mouth, hitting the back of my throat.

"Fuck yes," he hisses out. "Show me what you can do with that dirty mouth."

I want more than ever to pleasure Mark. I want to show him how much I care for him. How much his words mean to me.

My hand cups his balls as I slowly suck him farther into my mouth while swirling my tongue around him.

"Oh, fuck, baby. I'm going to come before we get to my apartment if you keep that up."

Sliding him out, I use my hand to rub up and down his shaft. My eyes move up his body, connecting with his.

When the elevator doors open to his penthouse, he pulls me up and throws me over his shoulder while he kicks our bags inside.

Walking into his apartment, he throws me off his shoulder, and I'm grateful my back lands on the plush sofa. Mark stands at the end of the sofa with his hand wrapped around his length.

"Take off your pants and spread your legs for me. I want to see that pretty pussy of yours."

Taking my time teasing him, I slowly take off my leggings. I didn't wear panties because they show a line, and I didn't have any clean thongs to put on, so I decided to go without.

Mark's strokes become harder, and I can see he's holding himself back.

"Open wider for me and touch yourself."

Spreading my knees farther apart, I ease my hand down, my touch whispering over my breast and stomach until my finger slides through my folds, landing on my clit.

"That's it, baby," Mark says with flames blazing in his ambers.

Not containing himself any longer, he climbs on the sofa, kneeling between my legs. His mouth has been on my pussy more times than I could count, but this time, it feels different. His words *I love you* keep playing in my mind. I can't help but feel a deeper connection with him.

His tongue slides up my pussy until he finds my clit. Biting down, he gives it just enough pressure for me to arch my back.

"You like that?"

I hum with appreciation at how well he knows my body. He places his mouth back on my clit as he dips a finger into me, curving it just at that right spot. My hands dig into his hair, encouraging him to be rougher. Biting me harder, I explode on his tongue.

"Oh God!" I scream out my release.

Mark moves up my body, placing small kisses on my skin until his lips are on mine and his tongue swipes inside my mouth. Never asking permission, always taking what is his. Letting me taste myself on him.

With one brutal thrust, he's inside of me so deep, I think he's pierced my lung because it takes all the air out of my body.

"You feel what you do to me?" I nod. "You're embedded in my soul, *M'Aingeal*."

Our lives may have been separate, but they were always meant to be as one. Every road I've taken has led me to the same destination. I'm meant to be with my Prince of Darkness.

CHAPTER THIRTY-THREE

Liz

The soft light in the bedroom lets me know it's morning.

There's a coldness in the air, making me shiver. The heat radiating from Mark's body isn't next to me, keeping me warm. Pulling the covers up to my chin to warm myself doesn't help. There's still something chilling me to the bone.

Deciding a hot shower would help warm me up, I toss the covers back, but when my feet hit the floor, I'm greeted with the cold hardwood. Taking a chance, I almost run across the room to the bathroom. Each step I take becomes colder and colder.

Walking into the bathroom, I turn on the hot water, shifting my weight from foot to foot so the cold tile doesn't cause frostbite on my toes. When the water becomes scolding hot, I shut the bathroom door to let the steam fill the room with heat.

The shower is larger than my bathroom and big enough to fit a party of five. There's so much more room, I can't imagine living in this type of luxury.

It's not long before the chill finally leaves, but I don't move. I stay under the showerheads, letting the water blister my skin.

It feels too good.

After a few moments of soaking my body, I reach for the soap bar, bringing it to my nose. Sniffing the scent of rainforest from the soap, I think about how much Mark smells like the fresh fragrance of waterfalls.

When I'm done lathering up my body and washing the soap off, reluctantly, I turn off the shower, grab a towel, and dry off.

Wrapping a dry towel around my body, I dial Rose. I know she's at work, but I've missed her and hope she can meet me for lunch.

"Liz!" Rose squeals.

"Rose, I've missed you." I'm just as equally excited.

"Blaze told me you guys came back with him. We need to get together soon."

"That's what I was calling about. I was hoping we could have lunch today. I don't think Mark came back last night from Red, and I don't feel like staying inside locked up."

"Hell, yes!" she yells into the phone. "Let me rearrange some things, and I can text you with a time. You have got to tell me all about you and Mark."

I almost want to laugh. Whatever this is between Mark and me is nothing like her and Blaze. They love each other, and it shines in their eyes. Mark and I have been fucking for years, and he's just now said he loves me. There's that little flip in my stomach thinking about those words again. I can't help but smile.

For the first time in my life, I want to tell Rose all about this fucked-up relationship between Mark and me.

***

I'm sitting at our favorite booth at Taco Mom's when a dark figure stands on the opposite side of the window.

I do my best not to turn my head to make eye contact, but

there's an uneasy feeling about the presence hovering over me.

"Miss," I call out to the waitress. When she walks over, I ask, "Can you tell me what the person looks like who's standing at the window?"

Her eyes move behind me, and she makes that look that says, 'you're crazy'.

"No one is there."

Spinning my head around, I verify what she's saying. My eyes search around the outside of the restaurant, trying to find any hint someone looks out of place. Nothing.

I know I'm not going crazy. I saw someone standing there. They were right beside the window.

Too scared to face them when I should have. I should've run outside and demanded they tell me what they wanted, but my fear took over, and my body couldn't react the way my mind was telling me I should.

A perky voice frightens me, making me jump out of my seat.

"Shit." My hand flies to my chest, holding my heart back before it jumps out and runs away.

Rose's arms wrap around me, pulling me into one of the hugs she's so known for.

"You scared the crap out of me."

"Oh." She laughs. "I didn't mean to." She looks at my face. "Liz," — taking a seat, she continues — "are you okay? Your face is pale."

"No, I'm fine. I was sitting here..." I can't help but turn my head to keep looking out the window. "Oh, sorry. I'm spooked. Someone was standing up against the window, staring at me. I was too scared to look to see who it was."

"You need to call Mark. He needs to know." Typical Rose.

She relies on Blaze more than I've relied on any man or anyone. I've never had someone look after me like Rose. I envy her life. She's always had people who cared about her, making a fuss over what she does. Blaze looks at her as if she's the only woman in the room. I know she deserves it. She doesn't have a selfish, spoiled bone in her body. She works hard, and it shows.

"No." I'm short when I say the word. "I'm sorry. I didn't mean it to sound harsh. I don't want to make a fuss."

"I understand, but he's not going to like it if something happens to you and you didn't tell him someone was creeping you out. Even if it is innocent."

She's right. I know she is, but this whole thing between us is new, and I want things to be normal for once in my life.

"I'll tell him." *Tonight.*

She gives me her stern look, as if I'm a toddler being bad.

"Okay, well, it's your ass."

Rose takes the menu off the table, pretending to read it.

We both know we'll be ordering the same thing we always do.

CHAPTER THIRTY-FOUR

Liz

After having lunch with Rose, I walked her back to work, not bothering to go inside the building.

Since it's nice outside, I figure I'll walk the rest of the way back to Mark's apartment, but before I do, I need to stop at the convenience store and grab a phone charger. I couldn't find mine, so I'm guessing I left it in Ireland. I won't ask his mother to send it because it costs more to mail than it's worth.

The wind blows slightly, and I catch the scent of bad body odor mixed with weed. *Oh God, that smell is awful.* It must be some of the guys down at the park. It's only a block over, and guys are always smoking what looks like cigars, but I know it's something else.

Heading in the opposite direction, the smell doesn't grow less in the distance, and I can't contain the chills running up my spine. My steps pick up, and I wish I would have just taken a taxi. When I round the corner and see the store come into view, I silently give thanks, but before I can make it, someone clears their throat, and when I turn around, I'm met with familiar eyes that will haunt me forever.

The buildings around me start crumbling, leaving me

wishing I was anywhere but here. I haven't seen him since the day I ran. I ran from him and my worthless mother and her endless drug habit. I've never not once regretted it.

His face looks aged, and the scar that runs from his cheek to his lip is a reminder that I fought him once. I can do it again, except I don't have a knife—this time.

"What do you want?" My words are harsh, but I don't care. I don't care what this man supplied to my mother or who he is in his low-life status.

He puts his rolled-up cigar to his mouth, takes a long drag, then slowly blows it in my face. Not wanting to give him pleasure, being overcome with the stench, I stand still, waiting for his reply.

"I think it should be obvious what I want," his raspy voice says as his gaze sweeps over my body.

"How did you find me?" I ignore the obvious. His eyes are filled with heat, and I want to run, but he's too close. After all these years, his presence still makes me feel insignificant, as though I'm a ball of nothing.

Drawing another puff and letting the smoke out, he grins.

"You didn't think you could run away, and I wouldn't know where you went?" He laughs, and it's chilling at how small I feel. Leaning closer to me, he continues, "You know your friend Carla was a good fuck, but I bet that sweet pussy of yours is sweeter."

The air around me becomes too thick to breathe. Feeling my knees about to give out, I stumble back. Somehow, I'm able to stand on my feet and pivot around, ready to run, only to take the first step before I'm yanked into an alley and thrown up against a brick building. I let out a scream, but when I turn, all I see is a hand bearing down, hitting me across the face and knocking me down to the dirty pavement. Sharp pain slices through my hands. Noises of scuffling fill my hearing. I need to get out of here, but I don't have the strength.

Oh my God, Carla. I'm so sorry.

She didn't deserve to have my fate. It should have been me instead of her. The pain I feel knowing my friend didn't deserve what happened to her fills my eyes, and the tears that escape are remorse for what she went through. It should have been my destiny.

I pull myself up using the wall behind me. What I see brings all my memories to the surface, and I run. I run and don't look back. I don't want to see them. I don't want to feel the pain of reliving the past.

Arms reach out to grab me, but I'm able to dodge them. I don't see who they belong to because I can't focus my sight from the tears that keep coming, but when they catch up to me and wrap around me, I know instantly they belong to the man who's my Prince of Darkness.

"Shhh, I've got you *M'Aingeal.*" His lips rest beside my ear. "It's okay, baby. It's okay."

Screaming with tears, I let it all out. My body shakes with waves of pent-up pain I've held onto it for way too long. I've built up a wall, caging it all inside. Mark holds me till the last scream, until the last tear falls, and I couldn't be more thankful because when the last tear falls, so does my body. I'm too weak to stand, so I let him scoop me up and carry me back to our home.

CHAPTER THIRTY-FIVE

Mark

Liz hasn't woken up yet. I had a doctor come to the apartment to check on her. He drew some blood work and told me he'd be in touch.

When Rose called Blaze to tell him someone was following Liz, I've never been so thankful for her loyalty to Blaze. I want Liz to rely on me like that. I want her to know I'll always be here to take care of her.

We left last night after Liz went to bed. We had to take care of Benny, who thought he was being a slick mother fucker to open a club up in Maine with the exact same details and layout as Red. The fucker. We've kept tabs on him, and thank fuck. With the loss of his hand, I'm sure it'll be a reminder not to take what isn't his.

We were almost back to Red when Blaze received that call, and my blood rushed to my hands, making them itch to get around the sick fuck's neck. When we arrived and watched to make sure the fucker wouldn't make a move, we didn't expect another man to jump to her rescue.

Blaze and Rose are here, along with Wilder, waiting for Liz to wake up. Wilder's wife couldn't make it; she's got all her little ones at home and is pregnant again. Fuck, Wilder's going to have a rugby team by the time Sarah is done popping babies out. I wonder how Liz would feel about having our own rugby team.

"So, let me get this straight," I say to the old man sitting on my couch. "You are Carla's dad, and you've been looking for Liz? Who is Carla?" I'm disappointed I hadn't known about this Carla. She sounds important to Liz.

The old man looks down to his lap, nodding. His face has a cloud of remorse hanging over it.

A soft moan fills the room from the doorway. Jumping from my seat, I run over to Liz. She's barely taken a step. Her eyes look up to mine and I can see pure love in them for the first time.

"Let me carry you," I bend down to pick her up and carry her to the oversized chair in the living room. Our eyes haven't broken connection, and when I set her down, she looks over to the old man. Her body stiffens, and her arms tighten around my neck.

"What… what is he doing here." Her voice is so low, I don't ever think she knew she spoke.

"He's the one who saved you. I was almost there, but then he stepped into the picture before I could get to you."

She looks at me like she needs confirmation. I give her a slow nod, letting her know it's true.

"Mr. Camp," Liz says to the old man.

I didn't bother asking him his name. I was too concerned about Liz when Blaze brought him. I wanted to thank him in person for saving my angel.

"I won't stay long, Liz. I wanted to say I was sorry for who I was back then. An alcoholic true to the bone. I didn't appreciate my Carla when she was here, and when she was killed, I made it my life's mission to find who did it and take their life. I know my actions were not the best, and one day, I hope you can forgive me." He stands and walks over to Liz.

I squeeze her knee, reassuring her I'm here.

"I wanted you to have this. It was Carla's mother's, then it was Carla's, but now it's yours." He hands her a small jewelry box.

Liz looks at it, and her hand shakily reaches out to take the box. Opening it, she pulls out a beautiful gold chain with a pendant of an angel.

"If you remember, Carla always wore it, except the night she was... killed." A tear slips down his round cheek, and he makes quick work of swiping it away. "Well, I'm off. I'm moving. I'm finally able to let go of the past. I hope you are too, Liz." He walks over to the waiting elevator and leaves.

Our eyes never leave the man until the elevator doors shut, blocking him from our view.

EPILOGUE

One Year Later

Liz

"Well, that is the last one," Mark huffs as he sets the box down.

God, that man is so fucking sexy. His t-shirt stretches across his chest, giving away all his defined muscles and abs. I can't help but gawk. I feel it in my core when he runs his hands over his chest to wipe the dirt off.

"You keep looking at me like that, and I'm going to put another baby in your belly," he teases.

He doesn't know he already has. Our son Mack is barely one, and now I'm expecting our second child. I planned on telling him on his birthday next week as a surprise, but I don't think I can hold off much longer. I'm growing faster than I did with Mack.

After last years attack I gave my notice to my job I

couldn't imagine going back to work and feeling safe in the community. My anxiety was just too high and it took to much energy trying to will myself to leave the apartment.

Even after a year and one baby later, I'm still glowing after Mark's proposal at Red. It was so special. He choose the same room he broke though my virginity barrier and took my innocence. The proposal will be a night I'll never forget.

After we decided to marry in Ireland Mark thought moving back to his homeland would be better for us to start our new life together and he was right. Everything came fast —marriage, the baby, then the move, but it couldn't be more perfect.

We lived with his family until we finally found something that wasn't too large but not too small and felt like home. The kind of home we can raise our children in. The best part is that Mark works side by side with his dad, and I work part time doing legal work for the brewery. I love being here. I love the fact that our babies will have loving grandparents to spoil them. My grandmother would be so happy to see how far I have come from the slums of New York.

After I told Mark who Carla was and what Mr. Camp had done, I had to beg him not to go after Mr. Camp. He was fuming, but what he did to save me from Jerry was heroic, and I couldn't let Mark go after him.

The day Mr. Camp left, that night, I dreamed of Carla. It was surreal. She told me to live my life without fear and that she wouldn't change anything. I needed to be happy and free of my past. She left me that night, and I haven't felt her presence since that day. Holding the necklace that hangs around my neck, I give it a little turn. It's a bittersweet memory of the friendship I lost that night, but it's also a reminder of the bond we shared that others rarely ever find.

The next day, the doctor called and said my blood work came back. I was pregnant. He wanted to do an ultrasound to verify, and we were to come in that afternoon.

Seeing the tiny human on the screen shifted something in Mark. He turned to me with an emotion of love and fear in his eyes and asked if I would be opposed to moving to Ireland so that he could work side by side with his dad.

The news that Mark and his family were working through their problems was like a lullaby to my ears. Too many years had passed between them without words, and being with his family would be the start of healing for all of them.

I was so happy to be leaving New York to start a new life without reminders of the struggles, especially for Mark to escape the underground life. I still think he takes part in some things, but I only have hope it's nothing like it was in the past.

Jacob comes around, and he and Caoimhe make eyes at each other, but any time Mark is around, they don't dare look in the other's direction. I've tried to talk to Mark. Caoimhe is a grown woman; if she wants to be with Jacob, that's her decision. She could do worse. Mark grunts and won't hear of it. I eventually stopped trying to get him to understand.

Unfortunately, Grace moved to New York to live in Mark's penthouse. She wanted a chance to start a new life independently after everything was out in the open. I want the best for my new sister-in-law. We talk once a week, and I can tell by her voice she's changing. There's an edge, a sharpness to her voice. When she mentioned that she'd been to Red, I saw a flash of something dark I didn't want to acknowledge because it would only mean that my beautiful sister-in-law has the same streak of being a nightmare my husband has.

They say things come in pairs, and I believe it. He's my Prince of Darkness, and I'm his Dark Angel.

****

Follow me on Amazon and subscribe to my newsletter to find out about new releases.
HTTPS://WWW.AURELIAYATESAUTHOR.COM/ NEWLETTER

ABOUT THE AUTHOR

Aurelia writes dark and contemporary romance and enjoys reading it just as much! She lives in Alabama with her husband, daughter, and fur babies. She spends most of her time caring for her loved ones and plotting stories. She's excited to share her stories and to grow as an author. Look for more outstanding stories from Aurelia by following her on social media.